LACE
K. C. WELLS

For Lynn

Good to meet you

♡ KC Wells

This is a work of fiction. Names, characters, places, and incidents either are the product of the author's imagination or are used fictitiously, and any resemblance to actual persons, living or dead, business establishments, events, or locales is entirely coincidental.

Lace
Copyright © 2017 by K.C. Wells
Cover Design by Meredith Russell

Cover content is being used for illustrative purposes only and any person depicted on the cover is a model.

The trademarked products mentioned in this book are the property of their respective owners, and are recognized as such.

All Rights Reserved. No part of this book may be reproduced or transmitted in any form or by any means, including electronic or mechanical, including photocopying, recording, or by any information storage and retrieval system without the written permission of the Publisher, except where permitted by law.

LACE

Thank you to my wonderful team – Jason,
Helena, Bev and Mardee.
And a huge Thank You to Meredith Russell,
who really outdid herself with the cover.

K.C. Wells

LACE

~ 1 ~

"You take sugar in your coffee, don't you?" Shawn called out as he spooned coffee into the mugs.

"Nah, gave it up," Dave called back. "I'm sweet enough."

Shawn smiled to himself. Never a truer word was spoken. Dave was *all* kinds of sweet, always had been since they were kids. Shawn's mum used to say Dave didn't have a mean bone in his body, and she had a point. Dave was the peacemaker, the one who could always see everyone's point of view, and as a result, everyone liked him.

Shawn *really* liked him, but that was another story.

He poured boiling water into the mugs, before reaching into the fridge for the milk. "You still haven't told me what you're doing here."

He caught Dave's snort. "Wow. Feeling the love. Do I need a reason to visit my mate on the weekend?"

"No, of course you don't." Shawn put the milk away. When he spied the packet of chocolate-covered biscuits standing next to the biscuit tin, he grinned. The way to a man's heart, and all that. And the way to Dave's heart was *definitely* chocolate.

Except his heart's taken, remember? Caroline? The receptionist from the gym?

Shawn didn't want to remember. Dave and Caroline had been dating for about three months, ever since Dave had taken the plunge and asked her out. Hence the reason why his visits had become more infrequent. Considering that he and Dave had previously spent a good deal of their weekends together, Shawn wasn't coping well with the separation. Of course, it didn't help matters that he'd been in love with his mate for virtually the whole time they'd known each other.

Not that I'm ever going to share that particular piece of information.

A lot of Shawn's gay friends often told tales about seducing straight guys, but that just wasn't Shawn. What made him even more sceptical was that a lot of their stories revolved around copious amounts of alcohol and subsequent loosening of inhibitions. When Shawn brought a guy to his bed, it had to be because they *both* knew what they wanted.

The thought made his heart sink. *And when was the last time you brought a guy home?* Long enough that he was thinking about buying shares in a company that manufactured lube…

Shawn pushed down hard on his brief flare of frustration, and carried the mugs and biscuits through to the living room where Dave was sprawled on the couch, shoes kicked off, long legs crossed at the ankles. *Fuck.* He had bare feet. There was something about bare feet that really pushed Shawn's buttons.

Except that bare feet could be added to a *list* of Shawn's buttons, and as buttons went, that was one of the more innocuous ones.

Dave craned his neck to look at Shawn, placing his phone face down on his belly. His eyes lit up. "Aw, choccy biscuits. Mate!" He scrambled into a sitting position and reached for the packet. "How did you know? God, I need a chocolate fix."

Shawn chuckled. "When do you not need a fix?" He put Dave's mug on the coffee table, before taking the armchair, curling up in it and tucking his feet under him.

Dave tore open the packet and the top biscuit shattered into a million crumbs all over his jeans, sprinkling themselves onto the carpet. "Fuck. Sorry."

"Leave it. I'll run the hoover round later."

Dave nodded and tipped what crumbs were left carefully onto the table. He took out a biscuit and bit into it. "Mmm, plain chocolate. My fave," he said around a mouthful of digestive. As he got another out of the packet, he sighed. "Can't remember the last time I had chocolate."

"Really? How many times have you been here and there *hasn't* been chocolate in some form or another?" Then Shawn smiled. "I forgot. You haven't been around here for a while." He kept his tone light. It was the closest he'd get to censure, and the moment he said the words, he feared he'd gone too far.

Fortunately, Dave appeared to have missed

that part. "Yeah, well, I've been watching my figure, haven't I?" he said gloomily.

"What the fuck for?" Shawn gazed incredulously at Dave's toned body, the well-defined arms, the muscled thighs encased in tight jeans. He knew exactly what that gorgeous body looked like—he'd seen it often enough when he accompanied Dave to the gym. Although he always made sure to avoid taking a shower at the same time as Dave.

Shawn didn't need any more torture.

"Had to keep in shape for Caroline, didn't I?" Dave huffed. "Not that it matters anymore."

Wait—what?

"Why not?" Shawn's heart hammered as his mind leaped to the obvious answer. *They've split up. He's single again.*

Not that either of those options did Shawn any good. There was no way he was about to make a move on his very straight best friend.

Dave shifted on the couch, until he was perched on the edge of the seat cushion, his hands wrapped around the mug. "We had a huge row last weekend," he confessed quietly. "Then she dumped me."

In spite of his racing heartbeat at the confirmation of his hopes, Shawn felt badly for him. "Aw, I'm sorry. But maybe you just need some time apart. Maybe you—"

Dave shook his head. "Nice thought, but it's not gonna work. Just leave it." He took another biscuit from the packet and gazed at it in appreciation. "Hey, at least I get to fill my face with choccy biscuits again, right?" He gave a half smile.

Shawn wasn't fooled by the attempt at humour.

"Wait a minute. You two were together for three months. That has to mean something, right? For all you know, this is just a hiccup," Shawn insisted. He loved Dave enough to want him to be happy, even if it was with a woman.

Dave raised his chin and looked Shawn in the eye. "No, mate. It's way more serious than a hiccup. You see, a lot of stuff came out last Saturday, and… " He shook his head. "Let's just change the subject."

Shawn was starting to worry. He regarded Dave closely. "No. Let's not. What stuff?" When Dave lowered his gaze, his face flushed, Shawn was intrigued. "Dave?"

Dave sighed. "I suppose I might as well tell you. Besides, the next time we go to the gym, someone's bound to tell you. Not like that lot to keep quiet when there's juicy gossip, right?"

Now Shawn's interest was well and truly piqued. "What… juicy gossip?"

Dave took a mouthful of coffee. "You see, the thing is… " Another mouthful of coffee.

Shawn had never known Dave to be so tight-lipped. "Hey," he said softly. "You know you can tell me anything, right? I mean, how long have we been friends?"

Dave nodded. "Yeah. I know. But this was sort of personal."

Shawn straightened, unfolding his legs. "Since when has something been so personal that you couldn't tell me?" The confession stung him a little. Dave had been the first person Shawn had come out to, back when he was fifteen. The one person Shawn confided in, trusted… loved, outside of his family.

Dave winced. "Look, Caroline was on reception at the gym the other day, all right? She came looking for me to ask me something. And… she found me… flirting with someone."

Shawn gaped. "She dumped you over *flirting*? That's a bit extreme, don't you think?" He peered closely at Dave. "Who were you flirting with?" He racked his brains to recall the other girls who worked with Caroline. Or maybe it was one of the women who used the ladies gym.

Dave groaned, put down his mug and cupped his head in his hands.

Okay, that was weird. "Dave? What's the matter?" For some reason all the hairs on Shawn's arms were standing on end.

Dave was still avoiding his gaze. "You know Jake? That guy who's always working out in the weights room? The one who watches himself in the mirror when he's lifting weights?"

Holy fuck.

"You were flirting… with Jake?" Shawn's jaw dropped for a second. "Since when do you flirt with guys?" No response. "Dave? Since when does a straight guy flirt with another man?"

Dave raised his head and peered at him through his eyelashes. "Since he discovered that he's not totally straight, but bi?"

Holiest of fucking Holy Fucks.

So many questions crowded their way into Shawn's mind. *How did you work out that you're bi? Are you attracted to Jake? Have you ever done anything with a guy?*

Of course, that segued into the most vital question of all.

Do you want to?

Sod's Law being what it was—an outright bastard—Shawn didn't get the chance to ask any of those all important questions, because that was the moment his phone chose to ring.

Or rather, his mother chose to call.

He gave Dave an apologetic glance, while holding on tight to the agonized groan that demanded to be set free. *God, her timing sucks.*

"Hey, Mum, what can I do for you?" Shawn kept his gaze focused on Dave, silently willing him to be patient, to not decide to leave—at least until Shawn had had the opportunity to ask what the hell was going on.

"Hi sweetheart, I know it's short notice, but do you think you could come round for dinner tonight?"

"Dinner?" For a moment the word didn't register, as if it was an alien language. *Dave has turned my brain into mush. That's what it is.*

"You know, that meal at the end of the day?"

He pushed out a low growl. "We've talked about you and sarcasm. You're not a good fit."

"Well, what do you expect when you say it in that tone? Anyone would think you'd never heard the word before."

He had to give it to his mother—sometimes her intuition was scary.

"Why the sudden invitation? I thought Saturday was your 'stay at home with a takeaway and watch Casualty' night." And *his* idea of the most boring way to spend an evening on the *planet*.

"Tonight's different. We've got guests coming for dinner, only one of them had to cancel, and I thought you might like to join us."

Oh God. Sitting around the dining table with friends of his parents. *Shoot me now.*

"Shawn?"

He tore himself away from what was turning out to be a very distracting conversation to find Dave stuffing his feet back into his shoes, before rising up off the couch. Shawn pressed his phone to his chest and whispered, "What's wrong?" *Apart from the fact that you just confessed to being bi-sexual.* His heart pounded. *Don't you dare leave. Don't you even* think *about leaving.*

Dave's face was flushed. "Look, you talk to your mum. I'll… I'll call you later, okay? I know you have a ton of stuff to do at the weekend." He left his mug of coffee on the table and grabbed his jacket from where he'd left it over the arm of the couch. "I'll let myself out."

Before Shawn could stop him, he was gone, the click of the door closing after him the only sound in the quiet flat.

Except for the muffled voice of his mother against his chest.

Shawn closed his eyes and counted to three. Slowly. Then he brought the phone to his ear. "Sorry about that, Mum. Dave was here but he had to leave." The reason for Dave's abrupt departure was bloody obvious. His best mate was embarrassed as hell.

"Aww. I didn't know. I'd have asked you to say hi for me. So, about dinner," she continued, with all the finesse of a steam roller.

"Sure. Fine. What time?" Shawn was in no mood to argue. He was still preoccupied with Dave's shock revelation.

"Be here for six, okay? That way, we won't be in a rush."

"Sure. I'll see you at six." He finished the call, his thoughts focused on Dave. *He's bi?*

Shawn wasn't an idiot. He knew it took two to tango. But it had to be something, knowing that both of them now danced to the same kind of music, right?

Right?

* * * * * *

Dave got behind the wheel and closed the car door.

Shit. I can't believe I told him.

He hadn't gone there with the intention of blurting out what had happened, but as usual his mouth had run away with him. And once the words had begun to tumble from his lips, he couldn't look at Shawn anymore. He didn't want to see what was on his friend's face, just in case it wasn't good news.

Wait a minute. Good news? Just what did I expect from him?

Then he snorted. Dave regarded himself in the rear view mirror. "Did you really think he'd think badly of ya?" This was *Shawn*, for God's sake. His best mate, through thick and thin. Maker of Mischief, Keeper of Secrets…

Except for the one secret Dave had thought too big to share—the reason why he'd first realized he might be bi-sexual.

When did it happen? When did my best friend morph into something different?

Dave knew that was bullshit. Shawn hadn't changed—this was all down to *him*.

I guess the question should really be, when did I start looking at my best mate like he was more than a friend? Because he'd never looked at Shawn the way he'd looked at him just now. And that phone call couldn't have come at a better time, because if not, Dave might have said something *really* stupid.

There was no way Dave was about to risk a friendship of so many years because he'd suddenly worked out he had the hots for his best mate.

Then it occurred to him that Shawn could look out of his window at any time. *What would he think if he saw me still here, talking to myself?*

Another snort. "He'd think I'd lost it."

Dave had a sneaking suspicion Shawn wouldn't be all that far off the mark.

Time to get out of there before he was spotted. He'd be back, of course. He'd have to apologize for leaving the way he did. Only there was another reason, wasn't there?

Dave needed to know something, before he really did go off his head.

Is this just me getting all mixed up—or is what I'm feeling real?

K.C. Wells

~ 2 ~

Shawn let himself into his parents' house and sniffed the air. Chicken, garlic, spices...

He smiled to himself. *Lovely. She's made my favourite—butter chicken curry.* His mum certainly knew how to spoil him.

Talk about a guilt trip. It had been ages since he'd been there. Not his fault—he'd only been avoiding it because Mum had an annoying habit of trying to fix him up with every stray gay guy who crossed her path. On occasions it had proved downright embarrassing.

"Hi, it's only a burglar," he called out. It was a standing joke every time he let himself in. Shawn had wanted to give back his keys, but Mum wouldn't hear of it. His argument that it was no longer his home fell on deaf ears.

"We're in the kitchen," Mum yelled back. From the living room, Shawn caught the sound of the TV, and he couldn't help chuckling. Guests or no guests, it seemed nothing would keep his Dad from his Saturday afternoon football. Shawn stuck his head around the door.

Dad was sitting in his armchair, slippered feet resting on Mum's tapestry-covered footstool-cum-sewing box, his newspaper spread out over his lap, and the largest mug known to Man beside him, full of tea. On the TV screen a match was drawing to a close.

Shawn squinted at the screen and groaned. "Aw, for God's sake. They're losing again?"

Dad groaned. "Not so loud. They might hear you." When Shawn frowned, he pointed to the screen. "They need all the luck they can get."

Shawn chuckled. "I doubt they can hear me through the TV, Dad." He inclined his head toward the kitchen. "So, who are the guests?"

His dad blinked. "Guests? There's only Tristan."

It took all of three seconds for Shawn to digest the information and arrive at an unfortunate conclusion. He recognized the name.

Judging from his dad's expression, he'd just worked it out as well. "Oh, Christ. She's at it again, isn't she? What did she tell you this time?"

"That I was making up for a missing guest." Shawn fought hard to keep his cool. The last time it had been on the pretext that someone wanted his accounting advice, except that the 'someone'—Ethan—had turned out to be Mum's new—and flamboyantly gay—neighbour. Shawn regarded his dad in dawning horror. "This Tristan... he's her hairdresser, isn't he? I'm sure that's what she said his name was. Is he like Ethan?"

Dad sighed heavily. "From the glimpse I got of him when he arrived, he could be Ethan's twin brother." He gave Shawn an apologetic glance. "I'm sorry, lad, but you know what she's like. She wants to see you settled down, you know, with a husband."

Shawn's sigh echoed his father's. "It's not *that* I mind so much, it's the type of guys she keeps finding for me."

Dad chuckled. "You know why, don't you? She always goes for the ones who are obviously gay. The ones she's not afraid of offending if she asks them."

Shawn snorted. "You mean the camp ones. There are plenty of gay men who aren't that obvious, you know." Then he started laughing.

"What's so funny?"

"Well, there was that one time, remember? When she asked the manager of the jewellery store if he was gay, and—"

"And it turned out he had a wife and two kids." His dad shook his head. "I think if she'd been a guy, he'd have decked her."

"Shawn? Where are you? Did you get lost on your way to the kitchen?" A couple of loud giggles followed.

Shawn exhaled loudly. "Oh well. No use putting it off, I suppose." He winked at his dad. "Wish me luck."

"Shawn?"

He paused at the open door. "Yeah?"

His dad grinned. "Be gentle with him. All he did was accept an invitation to dinner, remember? He has no idea about your mother's nefarious plotting."

Shawn pretended to consider it. "I suppose I can play nice. But if he's as obnoxious as the last one? The gloves are off."

Dad laughed. "Go get him. I'll have an ambulance on standby."

He chuckled. From the kitchen at the end of the hall, he could hear a lot of laughter, which boded well. Shawn took a deep breath and pushed open the door.

Mum was standing with her back to him, talking animatedly while she spread garlic butter over rolled out pizza dough, her version of garlic bread. Beside her was a tall drink of water with long, black hair that gleamed in the lights from above the stove. He was leaning against the fridge, in his hand a—

"Since when do you have cocktails in this house?" Shawn exclaimed, his head spinning. God Almighty, the number of times he'd suggested a cocktail he felt sure Mum would like, only to have her poo-poo the idea. And yet here she was, enjoying what looked like a Cosmo: her glass stood on the counter top.

Mum whirled around quickly, and a blob of garlic butter sailed from her knife across the room and landed on Shawn's black shirt. He gaped as the greasy concoction slid off the black cotton and landed on his newly cleaned, shiny black shoes.

Tristan stared for a moment, mouth open, and then burst into a torrent of laughter. "Oh *my*," he said, wiping his eyes.

Shawn arched his eyebrows at the pitch-perfect mimicry of George Takei. "So glad I amuse you," he said coolly. He inclined his head toward Tristan's cocktail glass. "I take it there's one for me?"

Mum blinked. "I don't even get a hug?"

"Only if you want to get garlic butter on your best blouse," Shawn said with a sweet smile. He walked over to her and kissed her cheek. "Hi. So when are the other dinner guests arriving?" He wasn't above making her squirm a little.

"Oh. Yes. Well." Mum giggled nervously. "Actually, it turns out that only Tristan here could make it. Plenty more for us, then."

"Really." Shawn folded his arms across his chest, careful to miss the buttery stain.

She gestured toward the oven, from which emanated the delicious odours that had held his nostrils captive since he'd entered the house. "I made your favourite," she said, smiling widely, as if this made up for the fact that she'd lied her arse off, and what was more, now realized *he* knew it too.

Tristan saved her from further embarrassment by pouring out a cocktail from the shaker and handing it to Shawn. "I hope you like Cosmos. I brought them with me."

Shawn paused, the glass a scant inch from his lips. "Them?"

Tristan nodded and grabbed a nearby can, holding it out for Shawn to examine.

"Cosmo in a can. Handy." Shawn took a sip and winced. "Bloody hell, it's pure sugar."

"I like it," Mum said brightly, her discomfiture forgotten. "You were right, you know, all those times you told me I'd love cocktails."

"Hmm, imagine that," Shawn murmured. "A gay man who knows about cocktails. That's right up there with queers who love show tunes, those who live for fashion and sassy sarcasm, and… " He couldn't resist. "What about that other oft-used gay stereotype that we know and love—the gay hairdresser?"

Tristan pursed his full lips. "Not *every* hairdresser is gay, you know."

Shawn took one look at Tristan's eyes, noting the mascara, then the regulation skinny jeans and tight-fitting T-shirt, and finally the smooth sheen of his hair. "Mm-hmm."

Tristan snorted. "I mean, if you'd just met me on the street, could you tell *I* was gay?"

Shawn blinked. His mum blinked. From their mouths came one word in perfect synchronization. "Yes."

Tristan opened his eyes wide. "Really?"

It was all Shawn could do to keep from laughing out loud. *He's got to be kidding!* Tristan was camp enough to set off every gaydar within a hundred mile radius. Then he realized he was *really* underestimating Tristan's range.

This is getting way too surreal. I'm gonna

need a ton more alcohol if I'm gonna survive this dinner.

Shawn downed his cocktail, wincing at its sweetness, and then held out his empty glass. "Got any more?"

Tristan's face lit up. "Sure." From a plastic bag on the floor, he pulled a couple of cans. "I've got Mojitos and Sex on the Beach."

"I'll have the sex, please," Shawn said with a grin, loving the gasp from his mum. He was past caring. Dinner had all the makings of The Meal From Hell, and he figured the more alcohol he consumed, the less likely he'd be to remember even one second of it in the morning.

* * * * * *

"That was delicious," Tristan declared, dabbing his lips with his napkin. "I would never have thought of serving pizza garlic bread with an Indian curry, but it just goes to show, I don't know everything." He put down his napkin and steepled his long fingers, the nails perfectly manicured.

Understatement of the decade was the first response to flicker through Shawn's mind. Instead he went with polite. "Actually, Mum makes it because it's my favourite."

Tristan beamed at her. "Aww, Sharon. You spoil him something rotten."

For some reason the comment stuck in

Shawn's throat, but before he could get a barb in, Tristan turned those big brown eyes on him. "So. Sharon tells me you're an accountant. That sounds… interesting."

Next to him, Dad winced.

Shawn snorted. "What you *really* mean, but are too polite to say, is boring." He waved a hand dismissively in the air. "You wouldn't be the first."

His response appeared to have emboldened Tristan. "Yes, well, since you said it first… " He laughed. "I mean, who decides that it's their dream to be an *accountant*?"

Across the table, Mum blinked, and then her gaze flickered nervously in Shawn's direction. Dad shook his head slowly, and gave Tristan a pitying glance.

Shawn had no such sympathies.

Okay. The gloves are officially off.

Shawn gave Tristan a sweet smile. "So, Tristan, you're a hairdresser."

Tristan flinched ever so slightly. "I prefer the term, 'stylist' myself."

"I'll just bet you do," Shawn said, making sure not to dim the wattage of his smile. "Do you own the salon?"

Tristan shook his head. "Marie owns it. I just started working for her last month."

Shawn opened his eyes wide. "Last month? My, you must have only just graduated from sweeping the hair off the floor. Does Marie let you cut hair, or haven't you progressed that far up the professional ladder yet?" He caught his dad's smothered chuckle.

Tristan's mouth tightened. "She says I might be cutting hair in a month or so. Right now I'm on blowdrying."

Shawn nodded sagely. "That means she has you working with all the pensioners, right? She's not ready to let you loose yet on the general public with a pair of scissors." Before Tristan could get a word in, Shawn leaned forward. "But you want to have your own salon one day, right?"

Tristan nodded eagerly. "That's my dream. I—"

"Well, when that day arrives, you're going to need someone like me, because without me, the tax man is going to take you for every penny he can. And it'll be someone like me who advises you on how to make sure that doesn't happen. Bet you won't think accountants are boring then, will you?" Even as he said the words, Shawn regretted them. He was being a first class bitch. Worse still, he knew why he was doing it, and it had nothing to do with Tristan.

It had *everything* to do with his mum interrupting what could potentially have been a really crucial conversation with Dave. It had *everything* to do with her trying to fix him up with any old boyfriend, when who he really wanted was Dave.

Tristan pushed back his chair and stood. "Excuse me, I… just need to go to the bathroom." He left the dining room in an awful hurry.

Dad coughed. "I think I'll just step out the back door and smoke my pipe for a minute." He gave Shawn a keen look before leaving the room. Shawn couldn't miss his dad's shaking shoulders as he exited.

Mum wasn't amused, however. Not in the slightest.

Shawn wasn't about to let her get in the first word. "You do *not* do this again, all right?"

She scowled at him. "Why are you so pissed off?"

"Why? Because you *keep* doing this. If I want a boyfriend, I'll find one for myself, okay? I certainly don't need my mother acting like some… " It was on the tip of his tongue to say 'pimp' but he reined in the impulse at the last minute. "Some matchmaker. I *am* twenty-seven, you know. That means I'm more than capable of handling my own life."

"Except you don't *have* a love life," she said quietly. "And why be like this now? You weren't this pissed off the last time I invited someone over."

He couldn't tell her truth, that he was taking his frustrations out on her. Because the person he wanted to be having dinner with was probably at the fucking gym, flirting with fucking *Jake*.

Mum's eyes widened. "Oh. I get it."

Shawn blinked. "You... do?" Shit, he hoped not. *Please, God, don't let Mum's intuition be scarily accurate.*

She nodded, her eyes shining. "You've met someone, haven't you? There's a guy somewhere that you're interested in."

"No," he insisted, although his heart was pounding.

She wasn't having it, apparently. "Don't you lie to me, Shawn Michael Collins. You're pissed off because I got you round here and you were too polite to say no, and there's someone you'd much rather be spending your Saturday night with. Tell me again that I'm wrong," she said triumphantly.

He groaned inwardly. Anything for a peaceful life. "Okay then, fine. Yes. There *is* someone. There. Happy now?"

"No! Don't stop there. What's his name? Where did you meet? Do *I* get to meet him?"

Shawn held up his hands. "Whoa. Slow down. Just because I'm interested in him, doesn't automatically mean that interest is returned, all right? And don't get your hopes up, because I really don't think anything will come of it."

With Shawn's luck, Dave was already on his knees in the shower at the gym, blowing Jake like his life depended on it. The thought made him feel sick.

Tristan entered the room quietly and retook his seat, clearly subdued.

And that's down to me. Shawn felt like such a dick right then.

When Tristan opened his mouth to speak, Shawn leaped in first. "Look, about earlier. I was out of line, okay? I'm sorry. I had no right to talk to you like that."

Tristan swallowed. "Oh. Okay. Sure."

He didn't *sound* sure.

"I tell you what." Shawn flicked his head toward the plastic bag containing the cans of cocktails. "How about we find some more ice, finish those cans, then raid my dad's drinks cabinet, so we can show my mum here how gay men make the *best* cocktails."

A slow grin spread over Tristan's face. "You're on." He glanced at Mum. "You are in for a wicked time. Well, depending on what's in the drinks cabinet." He winked. "Although if there's just a bottle of crème de menthe, we might have a problem."

Knowing his dad, that wasn't likely to be an issue. In fact…

Shawn smiled at his mum. "You *have* got painkillers in the house, right? Because come tomorrow morning, you are going to have one hell of a hangover." And with any luck, so would he.

Anything to wipe this evening from his memory.

~ 3 ~

Shawn folded up the last of his laundry and put it away. A glance at the clock beside his bed made him smile. *Plenty of time to go to the gym.* He liked his Sunday ritual. Up bright and early to get his washing done, then off to the gym with Dave to try and keep in shape. It wasn't enough, but it was something. Of course, the last three months had been a little different. Dave had actually been there, but only in spirit really. He'd spent his time talking with Caroline, keeping her company on reception. That was if he went at all. Sometimes Shawn would receive a text telling him his gym buddy was off doing something else.

Shawn had quickly realized that going to the gym alone sucked. He missed the banter between them, the competitive edge when they were in the weights room, the way they chatted while on the treadmill and the rowing machines. For him, going there was more than a means to get fit. For Shawn it was a social occasion, a chance to spend time with his best mate. And he felt the disruption to his ritual more than he could say.

Shawn pulled open the drawers to get out his gym gear and shove it into his bag, along with a towel for the shower. He needed a good workout. He'd spent more hours than usual at his desk the previous week, and his body was crying out for some exercise. Not to mention he had a hangover to work off. That just left a text to Dave, to find out what time they were going.

Hey. U going 2 the gym? U didn't say yesterday.

Shawn hoped they'd get a chance to talk, especially after the way things had ended on Saturday. *We need to get back to being us.* He wasn't about to get his hopes up: Dave's shock announcement did *not* mean he was suddenly about to declare an interest in dating Shawn, no matter how much Shawn might desire that very thing. No, Shawn would be perfectly happy if they could pick up where they'd left off, before Dave had gotten up enough nerve to ask Caroline out on a date.

Yeah, and that was weird. Dave wasn't the nervous type. And it wasn't as if he hadn't dated before. There had been a few girls on the scene over the years, nothing that lasted, sure, but enough to show he liked women. Except his previous girlfriends had been *nothing* like Caroline.

Shawn shook his head. Caroline was bold, loud, and sarcastic, with a body you couldn't help but notice. She kept in shape and was a great advert for the gym. And it had been clear from Day One when she first began to work on the reception desk that she had the hots for Dave.

She has good taste, that's why.

Dave was well built, with muscles in *all* the

right places, and just enough body fat that you knew he didn't eat, live and sleep in the gym. Shaggy black hair, the cutest nose, and bright blue eyes that never failed to send shivers down Shawn's spine. He joked to Dave about getting his hair cut, and yet what was really on the tip of his tongue was *Don't you fucking dare.* On those long nights when sleep proved elusive, Shawn would get out his Fleshjack, close his eyes, and imagine he was holding onto those shaggy locks while Dave's mouth was on him, sucking him deep, swallowing his dick to the root….

His phone pinged, shattering the extremely pleasant thought. One glance at the message had Shawn's heart plummeting.

Sorry. Forgot to mention I was coming early. Already here.

Shawn stared at the words, trying not to read between the lines, trying to ignore the hurt the message ignited in him. *He went without me. He didn't even call.*

Dave's message only served to strengthen Shawn's belief from the previous day. *He doesn't want to face me. He's too embarrassed.* It took a moment for another reason to creep into his mind.

He doesn't want me there because he's chatting up Jake, and I'd only cramp his style.

Yeah. *That* made sense. It was a week later, no Caroline in the picture anymore, and he could flirt with Jake to his heart's content. The more Shawn thought about it, the more he could picture it in his mind. Dave on his back, pushing weights, while Jake stood at his head spotting him, his dick tenting those loose-fitting shorts he always wore, the ones that made it *so* obvious he was freeballing…

Another ping broke his train of thought. *Want 2 join me? Almost done though.*

Shawn was nobody's fool. *If he really wanted me there, he would have asked before now.* Maybe Shawn's lack of response had sent Dave on a guilt trip. He didn't want that, not for a second.

Shawn's thumbs flew over the keypad. *Nah, we're good. I'll catch u another time. Enjoy. Work that body!*

Seconds later he had Dave's response. *LOL Will do.*

Shawn stuffed his phone into the pocket of his jeans. He knew he could always go to the gym on his own. But the thought of running into Dave, watching him shoot the breeze with Jake, watching the two of them circle each other like a pair of dogs in heat….

Whoa. Steady on.

He didn't know for sure that was happening, right? So what if Dave had admitted to flirting with Jake? That didn't mean he was doing it right that second. That didn't mean Dave had expressly *not* told Shawn so he could flirt without an audience.

That way of thinking was not good.

Shawn closed his eyes and took a moment to breathe, to regain his composure. *Just get on with your day and put him from your mind.*

Yeah. Like *that* was about to happen.

* * * * * *

Dave put his phone away and did his best not to think about Shawn. His chest tightened as he pictured Shawn's face. It didn't matter that Shawn was miles away—it was as if Dave could feel the hurt radiating from him.

I couldn't face him. Just… couldn't. Maybe in a week's time, Dave could put that whole conversation behind him, but right then it still felt too raw. Besides, being around Shawn just messed up Dave's wiring. He knew that after five or ten more minutes of talking, he'd have spilled everything—why he'd gone out with Caroline in the first place, for one thing. *Because let's face it, that had nothing to do with fancying her and everything to do with using her as some kind of a shield.*

Dave went to the lateral pull-down and attempted to shut off his mind, shut out the thoughts that had plagued him ever since he'd fled Shawn's place.

"So, about last Saturday."

Jake's deep voice filtered through Dave's consciousness, and he bit back a groan. *Oh God, no.* This was all he needed.

God apparently wasn't listening, because Jake was walking over to stand in front of him.

"Hmm?" Dave brazened it out, acting dumb.

"Did you say something?"

Jake quirked his eyebrows, and Dave could almost hear the unspoken question. *Are you shitting me?*

"I was asking about last Saturday," Jake said, lowering his voice. "Only, I've got a couple of questions."

No, no questions, Dave's brain hammered. *Please, Jake, for the love of God, just forget it?*

God still wasn't listening.

"So, was that you flirting with me cos you wanted to make the girlfriend jealous, keep her on her toes and send her a warning not to take you for granted? In which case it backfired big time, judging by the look on Caroline's face." Jake paused to take a breath. "Or was that you *really* flirting with me, because you've got the hots for me, you're genuinely interested, and that was your way of attracting my attention?" Jake grinned. "Cos I have to say, if it was the latter, it really worked." Jake winked at him. "And if what I've heard on the grapevine is true, then you're a single man again."

Oh God. Kill me now.

"Of course, you could have knocked me down with a feather when I realized you batted for both teams. I had no idea. You kept that close to your chest." He leered at Dave. "And such a nice chest too."

Dave had no clue what to say to him. He had a feeling that telling Jake no, he really *wasn't* that interested, that he'd simply been flexing his flirting muscle, wouldn't go down all that well. *How do I tell him that what I* really *wanted to know was if I was attractive to guys?*

It wasn't until he'd found himself telling Shawn all about it that he'd realized the truth.

He wanted to know if *Shawn* could be attracted to him.

And then I had to go and ruin it all by running like a scared rabbit.

"Dave?"

Hell. Jake expected an answer.

Dave took a deep breath. "Jake, I'm sure you're a great bloke, and—"

"And you can stop right there." Jake folded his arms across his wide chest. "I think I know what's coming. To tell the truth, I was a bit surprised when you started coming onto me."

"I wasn't exactly coming onto you," Dave muttered.

Jake snorted. "Bet that's not what your girlfriend thought, right? I heard she gave you a right earful."

That much was true. Dave sighed. "Sorry, Jake. You're right. I was flirting."

Jake stared at him. "So what was I? An experiment? Not that I'm complaining. You're actually just my type, not like some of the guys that come here. Take your mate, for instance."

Dave bristled at the implied criticism. "What's

wrong with Shawn?"

"I like my men with some muscle on them, something you can get hold of when it counts, you know. Shawn's okay, I suppose, he's just one of those slim guys who needs to work on his body a bit."

Dave glared. "Not all of us *want* to look like a condom stuffed with walnuts."

Jake grinned and flexed his arms, the muscles taut and firm. "But you like the muscles. I catch you looking. Come to think of it, I catch you looking a *lot*. You like looking at a guy who's all man." He chuckled. "That's why Shawn's your best friend and not your *boy*friend. He's not your type."

Dave was *this close* to flinging back at Jake, *What makes you think you know my type?* The arrogance of the prick. Dave *liked* the way Shawn looked. Okay, so he wasn't the muscular type, but he looked good. Short, sleek, dark brown hair, and deep brown eyes that always seemed to be sparkling and full of life. Yeah, he was slim around the waist and hips, but so what? He was most definitely all man, something Dave knew for a fact. He'd seen what Shawn was packing under his jeans and shirt. Showering after a workout was sheer hell: Dave would do his best not to stare, because he felt sure Shawn would have found that weird, but *damn*, that was one fine body…

The thought made him smile to himself. *Yeah, definitely bi.*

He gave Jake a smile. "You're right, of course. Shawn's not my boyfriend."

Not yet.

Maybe it was time to do something about that, when Dave worked up enough nerve.

* * * * * *

What are you waiting for?

Dave sat in his car, staring at the blue painted door that led to Shawn's flat. *This is getting to be a habit.* He'd arrived earlier than he'd intended, but that was due to the fact that he couldn't sit at home a second longer. He'd chewed things over for a whole week, and had *sort* of come to a decision.

I'm going to tell Shawn how I feel.

Except apparently it wasn't that easy. Shawn's blue front door was right there, and Dave still hadn't gotten up enough nerve to get out of the bloody car. They'd made plans to go out for lunch and then bowling, something they hadn't done for ages, but Dave was starting to have second thoughts. He knew he had to apologize, only the list was growing. He had the distinct feeling he'd put his foot in it the previous weekend. Shawn might have said he was okay about not going to the gym, but he'd been uncharacteristically silent during the past week.

So now I'm apologizing for running out on him last Saturday, and for being an arsehole on Sunday. Nice work, Dave. Maybe you can screw up this weekend too and make it a hat trick.

And then there was the matter of timing. When would be the right moment to tell Shawn what was going on with him?

He knew why his heart was racing. He really, *really* cared for Shawn, and the last thing he wanted was to mess it up. Because if there was just a *chance* that he and Shawn could find a little happiness together…

That did it. *Come on, man, grow a pair.*

Dave summoned up every last drop of courage and got out of the car.

* * * * * *

Shawn pulled the last load of clothing from the drier, throwing them in a heap in the laundry basket. Dave was due any minute, and he'd hoped to have all his chores done and dusted by then. He was still a little confused about the bowling part. *Bowling? On a Saturday afternoon?* It had been Dave's idea, and Shawn didn't have the heart to refuse him. He did consider the idea that maybe a bowling alley wasn't the best place to have a quiet chat, and that was probably why Dave had suggested it in the first place.

When the doorbell rang, Shawn swore his heartbeat sped up a little. After giving himself a swift kick up the arse for being so soft, he went to let Dave in. "Hey. Go on into the living room. I'm nearly finished dealing with the laundry." He didn't give Dave a chance to reply, but dashed back to the sanctuary of the kitchen.

"Are you sure you're okay to go bowling?" Dave called out. "I mean, if you've got stuff to do…"

Shawn paused in the middle of folding a T-shirt. It would be so easy to tell Dave yes, to call it off… except all that would be doing was postponing the inevitable. "Nah, we're good. I just need to put away all my clean clothes, and we can go."

"I'm sorry."

Shawn gave a start and turned around to glare at Dave in the doorway. "Jesus, make some noise before you sneak up on me like that. I could have had a heart attack." He went back to his folding. "And sorry for what?" His heart was pounding.

"Ducking out the way I did last week. I… I should have stayed until you'd finished talking to your mum."

Shawn forced a calm smile. "Hey, you had things to do. That was okay."

Dave shook his head. "No, it wasn't. And I'm sorry if what I told you was a shock. I shouldn't have blurted it out like that. It was probably embarrassing."

Shawn stopped folding and faced Dave. "Maybe I should say something here. It doesn't matter to me if you're bi-sexual." He winced inwardly when Dave stiffened. "Wait, that came out all wrong. I don't see you any differently because you're bi." That much was certainly true. Dave's sexuality didn't alter the fact that Shawn still had the hots for him.

"Really?" Dave's brow was still furrowed, as if Shawn's declaration hadn't eased his mind.

"Really. If anything, I'm glad if it means you're happier than you were before." Shawn's emotions were dangerously close to the surface. Another moment, and he would be telling Dave how he really felt. The possibility of sharing that information sent icy fingers crawling over his skin, and he suddenly had to get out of there. "I'll be right back." He made a dash for the bathroom, and once inside, the door closed, he leaned against it, his pulse racing.

Fuck. I am such a mess.

He ran warm water over his hands, his gaze fixed on his reflection in the mirror. *What would be the worst thing that could happen if I asked him out on a date? He might laugh at me? Tell me not to be so stupid?*

No. The worst thing would be if it altered their friendship irrevocably. If every time Dave looked at him in the future, he would recall that horrific moment when Shawn had had the nerve to think Dave could be interested in him like that, just because he'd come clean on his sexuality.

Shawn didn't think he could cope with that. It was best to say nothing.

There was also another consideration. *What if he says yes? What if it actually goes further than a freaking date? What if he finds out….*

Yeah. Keeping quiet was the best thing. Anything rather than see *that expression* on Dave's face, the one Shawn knew would be there as soon as Dave learned the truth.

Shawn dried his hands and exited the bathroom. "So, give me five minutes and we can—"

He was speaking to an empty kitchen.

"Dave?"

"In your bedroom," Dave called out. "Just thought I'd speed things along by putting away your laundry."

Damn, that man was sweet.

"So, do your briefs go in this top drawer?" Dave called out from the bedroom.

Shaun froze. *Oh fuck, no.* "Wait, don't go in—" He flung open the bedroom door and groaned inwardly at the sight that met his eyes.

Dave stood in front of the chest of drawers, holding up a pair of lacy white panties. He turned slowly to face Shawn, his eyebrows arched.

"And just whose are these?" Dave grinned. "Is there something you want to tell me?"

Fuck. Shaun's throat tightened.

Dave was examining the lingerie with interest. "Ooh, *very* nice. So I take it I'm not the only one with an announcement to make. Let me guess. You're not gay, you're bi, and you've got a girlfriend that you've somehow managed to keep a secret." He inclined his head toward the open drawer. "There's a hell of a lot of pretty underwear in here." He cocked his head to one side. "How am I doing?"

He… he thinks they belong to a woman? He thinks I'm bi?

Except Shawn knew he had to say something.

"You're not even remotely close. No, I'm not bi, I'm still gay. No, there's no secret girlfriend, and…. " He took a deep breath. "Those panties are mine."

~ 4 ~

Dave stared at him. Just… stared.

Come on, Dave. Say *something*. Shawn's heart hammered and his palms were clammy. No one—not a single living, breathing soul—knew about this, and what made it worse was that this was *Dave*, for God's sake. Shawn wasn't about to tell anyone in his family, because hell, there were some things you just didn't share, right? But Dave?

It was too late now. The cat was out of the bag.

Shouldn't that be the panties were out of the drawer?

It took a second or two for Shawn to realize that Dave had cleared his throat.

"So let me get this straight. *You* wear… panties." Dave's expression still registered his shock.

This was worse than Shawn had imagined. His balls felt like they were shrivelling up and retracting. *What else could I say once he'd opened the fucking drawer?*

He took a deep breath. "Yes," he breathed.

Dave's face was all kinds of scrunched up. "Why?"

Shawn took some small comfort in the fact that Dave wasn't running for the hills. If anything, it seemed like he really wanted to know.

Shit. How in the hell do I put it into words?

"Because when I wear them, I feel… different."

"Different, how?" Dave pressed him.

"Beautiful. Sexy." Shawn struggled to express himself fully. "I mean, what's wrong with wearing something silky and soft? Why should women be the only ones allowed to wear pretty, sensual things under their clothes? And that's a big part of it too. Knowing it's under there where no one else can see it? It feels forbidden and makes me feel naughty, not to mention sexy as hell." His heart no longer felt like it was about to explode from his chest, thank God. *He's still here. He's not looking at me like I'm some weirdo.* Come to think of it, the way Dave looked at him was sending heat rushing through Shawn's body, starting at his face and working its way south.

Dave's gaze dropped from Shawn's hot cheeks to the lace-front panties in his hands. "Sexy?"

In spite of his embarrassment, Shawn couldn't resist. "Yeah. It's hot."

Dave glanced down, the briefest of looks but Shawn caught it. *Holy fuck, did he just look at my crotch?*

Dave licked his lips. "So, does it make you feel good when you wear this stuff for a guy?"

Shawn blinked. "I… I've never worn this for anyone else. I buy lingerie because it makes me feel better about myself."

"And if someone *wanted* to see you in it?"

Breathing was suddenly a chore. *He did* not *just say that.*

"Someone?" Then his heart went straight back to pounding when Dave walked over to him, an unhurried, deliberate movement, the panties still in his hand. *What? What the....*

Dave stopped in front of him. "Me, for instance." And before Shawn had time to react, Dave leaned in and—

Shawn couldn't hold back his low cry of surprise when Dave's lips connected with his in a slow, gentle kiss. Then he pushed aside his shock to lose himself in the feel of Dave's mouth on his, Dave's hand on the back of his head, hesitant, like he was afraid that touching Shawn would somehow shatter him into a million pieces.

Shawn had to set him straight on that.

"Don't stop," he murmured into the kiss. Dave's soft sigh told him he'd said the right thing, and the kiss grew bolder, less chaste, more heated as Shawn opened for him. Then he froze when Dave pulled away. Shawn regarded him, his breathing shallow. "Did I move too fast?"

Dave smiled. "Sorry. It just hit me, that's all."

Shawn had a flash of insight. "You just realized you were kissing a man?"

Dave nodded. "Sort of overwhelmed me for a minute."

Shawn couldn't hold back his smile. "Maybe you need to do it again."

"More practicing?" Dave sighed. "I'm all for that." And then his lips were locked onto Shawn's, both hands holding his head, and Shawn could feel the silkiness of the panties Dave was still clutching.

Dave is kissing me. There is *a God.* Shawn slipped his arms around Dave's waist and held onto him, lost in this whole new world where the man he'd loved for so long was finally, *finally* making his dreams come true.

Well, one of them. Dave was interested. Dave was fucking *interested*.

Then his heart lurched when Dave kissed his neck, before moving up to his ear, his lips brushing over the lobe. "You don't mind then?"

"Mind?"

Another soft kiss to his ear, tickling him. "Me kissing you."

Shawn wanted to laugh. "You're kidding, right? I love it." The thought was right there in his head. *I've wanted to kiss you for so long.* Was it real?

"Thank God." Dave kissed his neck again, sending a shiver running down his spine. Shawn inclined his head to give Dave room, and Dave got the message. He planted gentle kisses down Shawn's neck, but then changed direction and headed north, only this time he sucked at the skin, making Shawn moan. "You like that?"

"Fuck, yes." Shawn still couldn't believe it. Dave was really kissing him. When he brushed his lips over Shawn's ear again, Shawn shuddered.

"So, do you think you could show me?" Dave asked in a whisper.

Wait… what?

"S-show you?" Shawn had to be hearing things. Because Dave could *not* mean what Shawn thought he meant. He could *not* be saying that he wanted to see Shawn in—

"Yeah." Another soft kiss to his ear. "I want to see you in these panties."

His heart was beating so fast, Shawn swore it was about to explode. The kiss had been enough of a heart stopping moment, but this?

"Are you wearing panties now?"

Holy shit. "No."

"Then put them on for me?"

But that would mean… Oh God. Shawn's heartbeat sped up.

"Shawn. Let me see you. Please." There was a note of urgency to Dave's voice that Shawn couldn't ignore.

He wanted to ask why. The question was there, *right fucking there*, only Shawn couldn't get the words out. Because deep down, the thought of letting Dave see him was turning him on. And the thought of what might follow was making him hard.

Shawn opened his mouth to say something, *anything*, but what came out was a squeaked, "Okay." Even as he said, he couldn't believe it.

Dave stilled. "Really?" He pulled back, his

pupils wide. "Fuck."

Shawn took a step back, his fingers trembling as he reached for the button on his jeans. "Sit on the bed." He couldn't do this when Dave was standing so close.

Dave didn't hesitate. He sat down, leaning back on his arms, his gaze focused on Shawn's waist. The panties were on the bed next to him.

Okay, this was new. Shawn stood there, heart hammering, his breathing erratic. *Think of it as a striptease. You've taken off your clothes for a guy before, right?*

Stripping for a guy who was about to fuck him was one thing. Stripping for Dave, simply because he'd asked to see him, was quite another. Shawn had no clue where this would go.

Keeping his movements casual, Shawn pulled off his T-shirt, because no way was he going to put his pretty underwear on while wearing a Hello Kitty shirt. He unfastened his jeans and pushed them down over his hips, revealing blue briefs that hugged his body. Of course, that might have had something to do with the way his cock was pushing against the soft cotton. Shawn ignored his erection and tried to unsuccessfully remove his jeans. It took him a moment to realize that he needed to take off his shoes first.

Dave, the swine, noticed. He smirked. "Don't give up the day job. You'd never make it as a stripper."

Shawn paid him no attention as he kicked off his shoes, followed by his jeans. It gave him no small measure of satisfaction to hear Dave's quietly murmured, "Fuck," when he slid off his briefs, taking his time, pausing when the waistband was low enough to reveal his pubes and the base of his dick. Another soft noise escaped Dave when Shawn's cock slid free of its restraints and bounced up.

God, that sound made Shawn feel powerful.

He took a step toward the bed, his hand outstretched. Dave gazed at it, his brow furrowed. Shawn smiled. "Panties, please."

Dave blinked, then reached for the lacy briefs. He held them out to Shawn. "Here."

Shawn took them, stepped back, and bent over to step into them. Slowly, deliberately, he pulled them up, easing them over the thick shaft that struggled to be contained. He couldn't help it. Putting on the silky, sexy lingerie always gave him a hard-on, but having Dave there, watching him do it?

Hotter. Than. Hell.

"Holy fucking God."

Shawn raised his head. Dave's gaze was riveted on him, his eyes wide. Shawn glanced down to where his hard dick pressed against the white lace front panel.

"Fucking hell, Shawn."

Shawn remembered to breathe. "You like them?" *I'm standing in front of Dave, naked but for a pair of lace briefs.* Certainly not something he'd ever seen coming.

"*Like* them?" Dave beckoned him with a crooked finger. "Come here."

Shawn stepped toward him, his heart pounding. When he was close enough that he could feel Dave's body heat, Dave looked up at him with a smile that made his heart beat faster, before bending lower and fastening his mouth around the head of Shawn's cock that poked up over the lace.

Holy fucking God was right.

Then Shawn forgot how to breathe completely when Dave mouthed his length through the lace.

His legs were shaking, and he struggled to remain upright when Dave placed his hand on Shawn's arse, sliding his fingertips under the silky fabric and squeezing his cheek. Dave's mouth was hot on his dick, his tongue flicking the head, sending shock waves of pleasure rippling through him. Shawn stared down at Dave as he stroked gentle fingers along his length while he sucked at the head. "God, look at you."

Dave paused in his sensual task and glanced up at him. "Can I take it out?"

The best Shawn could manage was to nod a couple of times.

Dave reached into the silken panties and pulled Shawn's cock free, easing the fabric under his balls and pushing them upward. He gave Shawn a smoking glance. "Fuck. You're really hard."

Shawn gave a shaky laugh. "And this surprises

you?" Heat blossomed inside him to see the hunger in Dave's eyes. "Go on," he urged. "Take me in your mouth." He could barely contain the desire that spread through him in a slow, pulsing tide.

Dave stared at the thick shaft, a bead of pre-come already at the slit. His gaze flickered up to meet Shawn's. "You know I'm wondering what that will taste like." Before Shawn could utter a word, Dave lapped up the clear liquid, licking his lips. Tentatively at first, he took Shawn's dick into his mouth, sucking hard on the head before drawing more of his length deeper.

Shawn's heart pounded, blood rushed past his ears and his belly quivered as he gently placed his hands on Dave's hair. Dave tilted his head up, Shawn's cock between his lips, Dave's eyes so dark and sexy.

"You look so good doing that," Shawn murmured.

Dave pulled free of his dick and smiled. "Not bad for my first time then?"

Shawn shook his head. "You could have been born to suck cocks." He didn't say the words he yearned to set free. *My cock, Dave. No one else's.* The thought of another man's dick in Dave's mouth made Shawn's marrow freeze over and his belly tighten. He stared down at Dave, willing him to hear the silent plea. *You're mine.*

Then Dave began to bob his head as he sucked and licked, and Shawn held Dave's head steady while he rocked his hips, keeping the movement gentle and fluid.

Only it didn't stay like that for long. Pretty soon Dave was moving faster, his fingers were digging into Shawn's cheeks, and Shawn's dick was dripping. The sight of Dave, his mouth working Shawn's cock, his shaft glistening as it slid between Dave's full lips, the feel of his hands on Shawn's arse....

Shawn had enough presence of mind to gasp out a warning before he came, but Dave didn't pull back, didn't waver in his task. If anything, he sucked harder, and Shawn had to lean on Dave's shoulders to prevent himself from toppling over, his legs trembling from the force of his orgasm.

When he was finally spent, Shawn eased his semi flaccid dick from Dave's mouth, and bent over to kiss him. The idea that he could taste himself on Dave's tongue, Dave's lips, filled him with a dark pleasure that sent shivers through him.

Dave lurched to his feet and Shawn found himself wrapped in Dave's arms, his mouth taken in another urgent, passionate kiss. Shawn went with it, melted into it, succumbed to the waves of pleasure that flowed through him and over him, crashing into him in a relentless tide.

"That was... wow." Dave shook his head. "No idea what came over me."

Shawn couldn't help stiffening. It wasn't exactly what he'd longed to hear, considering their activity during the last seven or eight minutes. What shocked him was that he let it go without comment.

Give him a break, okay? Shawn had to assume that was Dave's first time doing anything with a guy, and it had to be a big thing. *Let him process it. I mean, that's a hell of a lot to go through in a short space of time.* But he had to admit, the thought of going bowling was less appealing than the option of staying in and maybe making out a little.

Shawn found himself holding his breath to see which option Dave would choose.

Dave released him and grinned. "Time for me to wipe the floor with you. The ol' bowling arm is feeling pretty good today." He gave Shawn a quick peck on the cheek. "I'll let you get dressed. I'll be waiting in the living room." And with that he left the room.

Shawn stared at the bedroom door, his stomach clenching.

Well, fuck.

* * * * * *

"Hey!"

Dave emerged from his reverie to find Shawn staring at him, arms folded.

"Your turn, Dave. Bloody hell, you're really not with it today, are you?"

Dave got up hastily and went to pick up his ball. "Sorry. I was miles away."

"Hmm. Wherever this place is, you've been there most of the afternoon. We've barely spoken two words to each other since we got here." Shawn glanced at the scorecard.

Dave knew he was being a shit, but he didn't know what else to do. He'd feigned a jovial mood at Shawn's place, but once they were at the bowling alley, he'd retreated inwardly. He couldn't help himself. He had to think Shawn wouldn't know what to make of his near silence, but the truth was, Dave didn't trust himself to speak.

This was huge.

What bothered him most was the way he'd let lust take over, and that embarrassed the hell out of him. *Christ, I sucked Shawn's dick without even once telling him that I really, really like him.* Except he knew it was more than like. It just felt wrong to admit one week that he was bi, and for the next to be admitting to his best friend that he wanted to be more than friends, as if he'd only shared the former to be able to admit to the latter.

Of course, then there was the whole panties situation….

Dave couldn't deny it. The thought of Shawn in a pair of lacy panties had blown his mind. He'd held the scrap of silk in his hand and as soon as Shawn had revealed his secret, that was it. He'd seen Shawn's dick loads of times, but picturing it encased in silk and lace? Fucking hot. He had to see it. And of course, one thing led to another…

Then there was that whole mess inside his head to sort out.

Since he'd realized that his sexuality wasn't quite the fixed line he'd imagined, Dave had begun to notice guys. Not that he hadn't seen them before—it was just that now he was seeing them with 'Hey, they are really attractive' glasses firmly in place. The idea that he might end up having a relationship with a guy made him alternatively hot and cold.

Except Dave knew in his heart that he didn't want just any guy. He wanted Shawn. He'd look at the muscled men, the pretty boys, the good looking specimens around him, and yes, he'd imagined what sex might be like with any one of them. But Shawn? There was more to Shawn than mere sex. If *one* of those gorgeous guys had made a play for Dave, he'd have turned them down, just like he'd done with Jake. He'd always known sex was important to him in a relationship—hell, he and Caroline had burned up the sheets during the three months they'd been together—but with Shawn, things were… different. It took him a moment to realize why.

I already feel more for him than for any other person I've known. They had a deep connection. What shocked Dave more was that he wanted to pursue a relationship that wasn't based on sex.

And then I went and blew him.

Yeah, way to go to give the wrong message.

* * * * * *

Shawn had an idea why Dave was so quiet and introspective, one which he didn't like in the slightest.

One blow job had fucked everything up.

He'd spent all afternoon trying to figure out where it had all gone wrong, and he kept coming back to the *Shit, I screwed it up* theory. Except….

No. No. That doesn't add up. Dave kissed me. Dave was definitely interested. Dave made the first move. Dave wanted me to put on the panties.

No, it didn't add up, and now the question that tormented Shawn would not go away.

What did I do wrong?

He couldn't ask Dave outright. It was bad enough that Dave wasn't talking. Asking *why* he wasn't talking could only make things worse. No, it was obvious to Shawn that this wasn't going to work, no matter how badly he wanted it to.

All he could do now was hope that their friendship wasn't screwed up irrevocably.

Except I want to be more than his friend, damn it.

Shawn wanted to be Dave's *everything*.

~ 5 ~

U home?

Shawn stared at the message, aware of feeling torn. He hadn't heard a word from Dave all week, and for him to text now, after nothing, was…

Wait a minute. When did I ever hear from him during the week? They both had busy lives, demanding jobs. Weekends were when they got the chance to leave all that stress behind them and hang out together. *Why would Dave be texting me during the week to ask if I were home?*

And therein lay the problem. Dave was messing with his head.

Shawn knew what was bugging him. They'd shared an intimate experience, and then Dave had blatantly backed off. *He doesn't want that. He obviously crossed a line that he wasn't comfortable with, and he's backed off.* Okay. Shawn could deal with that. He might not be happy about it, but he was old enough and tough enough to suck it up and move on.

He just hoped things could go back to how they used to be, because the last thing he wanted was for Dave to feel so awkward around him that they couldn't stay friends.

That would be a tragedy.

Shawn let out a heavy sigh, and did what he'd

always known he'd do. *Yes. U want to come round?*

On my way.

No hesitation, not for a second. The speed of Dave's response made him feel a little better. Maybe things weren't as bad as he'd thought.

Shawn picked up his empty plate from the coffee table and carried it through to the kitchen. He'd planned on watching a film he'd recorded a few nights ago, but it could wait. He had to admit, he was curious to see how Dave behaved. Would he make any reference to what had happened? Would he mention Shawn's little… kink? That was the part that had given Shawn more than a few pangs the last few days. Of all the people to learn his secret, why did it have to be Dave?

The doorbell chimed, and Shawn gave a start. *What, already?* He stepped into the tiny hallway and peered through the lens. Yeah, it was Dave. Shawn opened the door, a smile in place. "What did you do, text me from around the corner?"

Dave gave him a sheepish glance. "Yes, actually. I was hoping you were in." He stilled. "It *is* okay to stop by?"

Shawn decided right there and then that he did *not* like this newfound reticence. That wasn't like Dave at all. "Of course it is. I'd have said if it wasn't. Now get your arse in here."

Dave laughed, and just like that the stiffness across his shoulders was less evident. He stepped into the flat, a plastic carrier bag in his hand. "So what are you up to this evening?"

"I was going to watch a film. I have wine and snacks. Interested?" Shawn didn't mind the idea of Dave keeping him company. Not one bit.

Dave gave him a keen focused glance. "That depends. What kind of film are we talking about?"

Shawn chuckled. "Wow. Anyone would think I was going to tie you to my armchair and subject you to hours of Open University documentaries. It's only a James Bond one, Skyfall. Have you seen it?"

Dave smiled broadly. "Yeah, but I wouldn't say no to seeing it again. Got enough wine for two?"

Shawn merely arched his eyebrows to let Dave know that some questions were just plain stupid. "Go on into the living room. I'll bring the wine, glasses and snacks through." He waited until Dave had left him, then let out a long exhale. He didn't know whether to be disappointed or relieved that Dave appeared so… normal. Then he decided he could live with it, especially if it meant things got back to how they used to be.

Shawn carried in a tray bearing a cold bottle of white wine, two glasses and a bowl of crisps and cheesy snacks. Dave dove right in, and Shawn had to laugh. "Did you not eat tonight or something?"

Dave stared at him, his cheeks bulging, looking for all the world like some crazed hamster. He tried to say something, but only ended up spraying Shawn, the couch and the carpet with bits of corn chips.

"Ew. Empty your mouth first." Shawn shook his head at the sight of bits of soggy yellow snack on the carpet. "Anyone would think you weren't house-trained." He went into the kitchen, returned with a roll of paper towels, and thrust it into Dave's hand. "Here. Clean up your mess."

Dave's face fell, and he knelt on the carpet to do as instructed. Shawn tried not to smile, but really, Dave's muttering under his breath was adorable.

"Sorry, I didn't catch that. Did you say something?"

Dave raised his head. "I said, this wasn't exactly what I had in mind when I came round here tonight." He got to his feet and took both the roll and his screwed up wads of towel into the kitchen. Shawn watched him go, his pulse picking up a little speed. Suddenly he wanted to know more.

He unscrewed the cap off the bottle and poured out two glasses.

"Wow. No corks. Must be the good stuff." Dave stood beside the couch, smirking.

Shawn gave Dave a pointed look. "It's better than that shit you brought to my parents' barbecue last summer. You remember, the bottle of wine that you opened and instead of pouring it out, you drank the whole thing through a straw?"

Dave winced. "I don't recall what the wine was, but I sure as hell remember the hangover the following day." He sat on the couch and took a drink from his glass.

Shawn joined him, picking up his own glass. For some reason he felt nervous. "Ready for the film?" Anything to avoid any awkward silences.

"Can… can I say something first?"

"Sure." Shawn's heartbeat shifted into a higher gear, and he tightened his hold on the slender stem of the wine glass.

"About last Saturday. I… I'm sorry about how I was." Dave was avoiding Shawn's gaze.

"Oh? And how were you?" It seemed such a nondescript thing to say.

"I shouldn't have let myself get carried away like that. Anyone would think I'd never seen lingerie before."

Shawn chuckled, partly to lighten the mood, though more to mask his own nervous state. "Yeah, well, you're probably used to seeing it on your girlfriends or on those mannequins that you see in the department stores. You know, the ones that all have the same cup size?"

Dave flashed him a sudden grin. "Oh? And what's your cup size?"

Shawn kept his face straight. "Rolled up gym sock."

Dave burst out laughing. "God, now *that* is something I'd love to see." Shawn joined in, but then the laughter died away when Dave speared him with an intense gaze. "Only, I'm not joking. I bet you'd look amazing in a basque or a teddy."

Holy hell, he's serious.

Shawn didn't know how to react, but then the moment passed when Dave reached down to where he'd left his plastic bag. He picked it up and handed it to Shawn. "Here. I bought you something."

It wasn't until the bag was in his possession that Shawn noticed both their hands were trembling. He pulled a plain white box free of the bag and set it down on his lap, staring at it.

"Well? Aren't you going to open it?" Dave demanded.

Shawn took a deep breath and opened the box. A layer of tissue hid its contents from view, and he lifted up the pretty paper with its tiny rosebuds and saw…

Oh. Wow.

"I… don't know what to say." Beneath the tissue lay two pairs of briefs. Shawn lifted the top pair and gazed at the gauzy black panties. They were sheer, with flowers embroidered on the front, the back plain. Shawn imagined how his dick would look through the filmy fabric, and just like that, his cock half filled. The second pair was actually a thong. The front was done in white with teeny tiny polka dots and a frill along the leg edge, but the back… Floral lace started out narrowly at the hips, flowing down to peter out in a thin string.

"Well? Do you like them?"

Shawn interrupted his admiration of the lovely items and stared at Dave. "They're beautiful. Thank you."

Dave gave him a sheepish smile. "I have to say, ever since I saw you in those panties, I couldn't get you out of my mind. Though I was worried that they might not fit. I kind of had to guess at the size." He frowned. "Is that a problem? Finding stuff that will fit your... package?"

Shawn grinned. "Would you believe there are online sites which cater for guys?"

Dave's eyes opened wide. "Seriously?"

He nodded. "Lingerie designed with men in mind. Which is wonderful, because some of the things I see in the shops are damned uncomfortable."

"Will these fit, do you think?"

Shawn loved the note of concern in Dave's voice, the hint of anxiety. "I'm sure they'll fit just fine." Then he recalled the way Dave had looked at him the previous weekend, the way he'd licked his lips when Shawn had faced him, the white lace moulding itself to his erect dick. Shawn's heart pounded. "Why don't we find out?"

Dave blinked. Blinked again. "But... you haven't finished going through the box yet."

Wait... what?

Shawn peered into the box and lifted up yet another layer of tissue. Below it lay a garter belt that matched the black pair, and....

Holy Mother of God.

"I wasn't sure if you wore stockings. I... I didn't look that closely into your top drawer."

Shawn was silent as he placed the panties on

the arm of the couch, and picked up the sheer black stockings with lacy tops. They felt like silk against his fingers, gossamer soft.

"You don't like them." Dave's voice was flat.

Shit. Shawn heaved a sigh. *I'm making a real mess of this.* He knew what he wanted right then, he just didn't know if he had the nerve to go for it.

"Yes, I wear them. I don't go out in them, but I do wear them sometimes in my bedroom. And I love them. They're gorgeous." Shawn placed them back in the box and then laid the panties on top of them. He held out a hand to Dave. "So why don't we go to my bedroom where I can show you how much I appreciate your gift?" His heart hammered, and inside his belly was a writhing mass of nervous tension as he awaited Dave's response.

Dave regarded his extended hand, his eyes so dark, sitting there so damn still…

Then he rose to his feet and grasped Shawn's outstretched hand. "I think I'd like that very much." There was a slight quaver in his voice.

Fuck. Fuckityfuckfuck. Shawn was suddenly in unfamiliar territory. Because it felt like Dave was on the same page.

He led Dave out of the living room and into his bedroom. When Shawn placed the white box on the bed, Dave stepped in close. "Shawn? There's just one thing…"

Shawn's stomach was churning. *He's having second thoughts. He's changed his—*

"Turn your phone off or put the damn thing on silent." Dave's eyes danced with amusement. "Because I don't think either of us want to be disturbed right now by a phone call from your mum."

Shawn laughed. "Good thinking." He pulled his phone from his pocket and switched it to silent. His pulse raced when Dave took the phone from his hand and placed it on the bedside table. He walked back to where Shawn stood, reached out to cup his head, and drew him closer into a gentle kiss.

God, Shawn had missed those lips. He looped his arms around Dave's neck and returned the kiss, parting his lips when Dave's tongue demanded entrance. Shawn lost himself in the kiss as he stroked Dave's nape and ran his fingers through his hair. When Dave brushed his fingers over Shawn's chest, his nipples grew taut beneath the cotton, pushing against it and making him shudder.

"God, you're a great kisser," Dave murmured against his lips.

Shawn sighed with pleasure. "Well, look what I get to work with." He couldn't get enough of that mouth, those soft, full lips, that eager tongue. Then Dave made his heart beat faster when he slid his hand lower, until it reached his jeans. Shawn held his breath as Dave cupped his burgeoning erection. When he finally got his breath back, Shawn said quietly, "See? That's what your kisses do to me."

"I want to see you in your presents." Dave's

gaze locked onto his. "Naked, except for panties, a garter belt and stockings."

Shawn's heart was beating so strongly, he felt sure Dave could hear it. "Okay." The word came out as a whisper. Here he was, twenty-seven years old, and Dave's kisses and sensual words had taken him right back to his first time, a nervous virgin who was so turned on, he'd felt like the lightest touch would have him coming.

He took a step away from Dave and began to undress, his hands shaking as he removed his T-Shirt. Something inside Shawn told him this was going to be more than a blow job. As if in response to his unspoken thought, Dave grasped the hem of his own T-shirt and pulled it up and over his head, revealing the wide chest Shawn knew so well.

Don't stare. Don't stare.

But he couldn't help it. He longed to trace a line between Dave's nipples with his tongue, to tweak them until Dave moaned with pleasure. He wanted to—

"More skin, Shawn."

Dave's amused remark cut through the fog of desire that clouded Shawn's mind.

Shawn decided Dave was way too calm, too smug. He grinned. "I think I need some help here."

"Oh?" Dave arched his eyebrows. "What's giving you problems?"

"My jeans. I might need you to help me take them off."

Dave's sexy smile was doing things to Shawn's insides. *Does he know the effect he has on me?* Then Shawn bit back a groan as Dave slowly unfastened the button on Shawn's waistband. *Yeah, he knows exactly what he's doing, the fucker.*

Having Dave look him in the eye while he slowly lowered the zipper on Shawn's jeans was probably the hottest thing to happen to him in a long while. And the fact that his gaze didn't waver when he slipped his hand inside to graze the head of Shawn's dick with his fingers, succeeded in ramping up Shawn's need from *fuck yes* to *Oh My Fucking God.*

"Yeah, I can see why these might give you problems." Dave had never sounded so husky. Then he grabbed hold of the waistband with both hands and gave an almighty tug, pulling them down roughly over Shawn's hips.

Shawn froze for a second, and then the two of them battled with each other's clothing in between heated kisses and stumbling into one another as they squirmed out of jeans and underwear. Shawn was in no doubt as to what was coming, and his heart pounded as Dave's glorious body was revealed. This time Shawn made no attempt to avoid looking at Dave's cock, and he was pleased to see his bold glances hadn't gone unnoticed. Dave shivered, but he straightened, his cut dick already at half-mast.

Shawn couldn't resist. He reached down to wrap his fingers around Dave's length, and was rewarded when it hardened further, a column of hot flesh that Shawn desperately wanted inside him. Dave closed his eyes, his breathing quickening.

"Does it feel good when I touch you?" Like Shawn couldn't tell the answer to that, but he wanted to hear the words.

"God, yeah," Dave whispered. When Shawn gently caressed him from root to head, Dave shuddered. "Feels... different."

"A good different?"

Dave's eyes popped open and he smiled. *Fuck, the light in those eyes...*

"A very good different." Then Dave stayed Shawn's hand. "But now I want to see you." He took a step back and climbed onto the bed, shuffling backward until he was leaning against the mound of pillows. Dave reached down and languidly stroked his dick. He nodded his head toward the box.

His fingers trembling, Shawn picked up the black panties and stepped into them carefully. He pulled them up over his thighs and hips, the fabric barely covering his erect cock.

"Fuck. Have you any idea how sexy you look in those?" Dave sounded hoarse.

"Tell me." Shawn stood still, feet slightly apart, his hands by his sides. Slowly he turned, making sure Dave got a good look.

"Oh, Christ. I can see your crack through them. God, they're so sheer."

Shawn faced him again. "And now?" He felt

amazing, more alive than ever before.

"Fuck, the way they make your cock look."

Shawn didn't have to look. He could feel how his dick pushed at the flimsy lingerie. He picked up the garter belt, fastened it around his waist, then sat on the edge of the bed while he slipped his hand inside one of the sheer stockings.

"I want to watch," Dave demanded.

Shawn shifted on the bed until he was at Dave's side, then he eased his foot into the fragile stocking, gently unrolling it until the lace top was at his thigh.

Before he could snap the fasteners into position, Dave knelt up. "Let me."

Shawn bent his leg and held his breath as Dave stroked up his leg, his fingertip grazing the silken stocking until he reached the lacy top. He secured the fastenings and then sat back on his haunches. "Now the other one."

Shawn repeated the process until at last he was done, his legs encased in a sheer layer of black silk. His pulse raced as Dave edged closer, his hand curling around Shawn's nape, pulling him into a kiss.

"You look amazing," Dave murmured against his lips, before taking his mouth in a hot kiss. Shawn closed his eyes as Dave kissed his neck, moving lower to his chest. Fuck, Dave's hands were everywhere, on his nape, his shoulders, stroking his belly, like he couldn't stop touching Shawn. He moaned when Dave's lips met his, and their tongues duelled in a sensual battle.

Making out had never been like this, as if all his senses were heightened. Shawn was hyper aware of every touch, every caress, every noise that left Dave's lips, the way he smelled, a warm, spicy scent that crept into Shawn's nostrils.

And those kisses. It was as if Dave couldn't stop, as though he were irresistibly drawn to Shawn's mouth, unable to refrain from kissing him for more than a couple of seconds.

Shawn was in heaven. For him, kissing was an intimate act to be savoured, and to find a partner who clearly enjoyed it as much as he did was even more of a turn on.

Then Dave broke the kiss and moved lower to flick Shawn's nipple with his tongue.

Shawn shivered and pushed his head back into the pillows, arching his body as if to demand more. Dave's hands were all over him, stroking him through the flimsy panties, tracing the outline of his dick. He stroked the tops of Shawn's thighs above the lace of the stockings, making the muscles jump in Shawn's inner thighs.

"Let me make you feel good too," Shawn whispered. He stroked Dave's chest, feeling the warm skin pebble beneath his fingertips. "Do you like that?"

Dave's only response was a long, drawn-out sigh when Shawn slid his hand lower to stroke his cock. His breathing grew loud and rapid, and he pressed his face against Shawn's chest, his breath hot.

"I'll take that as a yes." Shawn flipped Dave until he lay on his back, his dick rigid as he pulled Shawn into another kiss.

Much as Shawn loved those kisses, he had something else in mind. Dave's mind, to be exact, and Shawn was about to blow it.

He broke the kiss and bent his head to lick Dave's nipple with a languid tongue while he reached lower to mould his hand around Dave's heavy cock. Dave let out a soft gasp, and his face bore an expression of astonishment, as though he hadn't expected it to feel this good.

Shawn was more than happy with that reaction. He flicked at the taut nub, before tugging on it gently with his teeth. Dave closed his eyes and groaned, hips rising up from the bed as he pushed his cock into Shawn's hand. Shawn traced a line between his nipples, bestowing the same attention on the other, before alternatively kissing and licking his way down Dave's sternum, over his abs, until Dave's pubes were right there, inches from his mouth.

Shawn paused and raised his head, seeking Dave's gaze. His dark eyes were focused on Shawn's face, searching it, almost as if he was checking that this was really happening. Shawn gave him a warm smile, and finally, *finally* got his mouth right where he wanted it.

He took Dave's dick deep, working it with his tongue, licking up and down its stony length, sucking hard on the wide flared head while he cupped Dave's balls.

"Christ!" Dave was panting, hips rolling up off the bed, his eyes closed, and for a brief moment it crossed Shawn's mind that maybe he found it easier like that, when he couldn't see who was blowing him. But Dave shot that theory all to hell when he opened his eyes and stared into Shawn's, nodding. Shawn took that as permission and began to bob up and down on Dave's cock, thrilled to feel Dave's hands on the back of his head, holding him there while Shawn sucked and licked that glorious dick, rubbing his thumb over Dave's balls.

When Shawn paused to take a breath, Dave made a move. He flipped them until Shawn lay on his back, Dave on top of him, their mouths reconnecting in kiss after kiss. Shawn slipped his hand under the filmy fabric, stroking his cock, but Dave broke the kiss and shook his head.

"That's mine." The huskiness in his voice sent shivers coursing through Shawn. Dave was on all fours over him, his gaze focused on Shawn's crotch. "Can… can I fuck you?"

Shawn shuddered. Fantasizing about hearing those words from Dave's lips was one thing. Actually hearing them was fucking *hot*. Desire robbed him of speech, and all he could do was nod.

He hooked his thumbs under the elasticated waist of his panties to slip them off, but Dave shook his head once more. "Leave them on. All of it."

Oh God. It was as if Dave had delved into the deepest, darkest reaches of Shawn's mind and pulled his most delicious fantasy into the light. His breathing quickened as Dave stroked his cock through the panties, before grasping one side and pulling the fabric over to the other, freeing Shawn's rock hard dick that poked out from beneath the sheer black layer. Dave lowered his head to lick the length of it, and Shawn let out a low hum of pleasure. Obviously encouraged, Dave sucked the head into his mouth and worked it, sliding his lips down the shaft.

It was exquisite torture, and Shawn wanted more. "Please… please…."

Dave pulled free, his chest rising and falling rapidly. He shifted position until he lay next to Shawn, who was half on his side. Dave tucked in behind him, his cock hot and heavy against Shawn's body. Dave caressed the top of Shawn's thigh where the lace ended, the muscles there jumping as Dave stroked inward, his fingers tracing the outline of Shawn's balls through the panties.

"Where's the lube?" Dave whispered into Shawn's ear.

Shawn didn't waste a second. He stretched out a hand toward the bedside table and yanked open the drawer. When his fingers came into contact with the bottle, he grasped it and almost flung it across the bed, where it landed between his parted thighs.

Dave snickered. "Anyone would think you were eager for this."

Shawn locked gazes with him, saying nothing, but hoping to God his expression conveyed the white-hot need within him. Dave's only response was to tug at the panties, pulling them to one side. "Grab hold of your leg," he demanded.

Shawn did as instructed, lifting it toward his chest. The next thing he felt was Dave's slick finger penetrating him slowly. "Oh, fuck."

Dave leaned over to kiss him. "Not my first time fucking someone's arse. I know what to do, okay? Have to get you ready." He grinned. "I'm not exactly small." He pushed deeper into Shawn's body, and Shawn groaned at the welcome intrusion. Dave moved in and out a few times before adding another.

Shawn couldn't wait any longer. "Want you inside me." He didn't take his gaze off Dave.

Those long fingers stilled. "Fuck," Dave exclaimed, withdrawing them, then wiping them over his dick. He bent over to kiss Shawn, a lingering, thorough kiss that made Shawn yearn for more, and suddenly he could feel the head of Dave's dick pressing unhurriedly into him.

Bloody hell. He was bare.

"Wait." Shawn froze, and Dave was quick to react, stilling instantly, the head *right there*.

"What's wrong?"

Shawn swallowed. "You're not wearing a condom."

An agonized expression crawled across Dave's face. "Do... do I need one? I mean, I had my last work physical two weeks ago. I got a clean bill of health and I haven't been with anyone since." His eyes widened. "Unless.... "

Shawn shook his head vehemently. "I'm the same. I get tested regularly, and there hasn't been anyone for... well, months."

Dave rolled his eyes. "Then for fuck's sake, tell me I can keep going. Because right now my cock is aching to be inside you."

God. I want that too.

Shawn scanned that face he loved so much, those dark eyes regarding him earnestly. "I've never.... " he began. Then he stopped. This was *Dave*, for God's sake, the man Shawn had loved since he was sixteen. The man he'd trust with his life.

One hand still holding onto his leg, Shawn cupped Dave's cheek with the other and looked into his eyes. "Fuck me," he said, his voice steadier than he'd thought possible under the circumstances.

Dave's breathing sped up and slowly, so exquisitely slowly, slid into Shawn's tight hole, his mouth open as he filled Shawn to the hilt, an expression that was almost awe on his face. He closed his eyes, but Shawn wasn't having that. He wanted Dave to be aware of *everything*.

"Look at me," he whispered.

Dave opened his eyes and met Shawn's gaze.

Shawn smiled. "You feel amazing inside me. Now move."

Apparently it was all Dave needed to get him going. He slid into Shawn, his cock brushing against the silken panties still clutched in his hand. "You look so fucking sexy like this," Dave gasped out, picking up speed. He kissed Shawn's leg, before stroking the bare strip of flesh above the stocking tops.

Shawn had never felt sexier. He arched into Dave's touch, moaning softly when Dave leaned over to kiss his nipples, his chest, his cock gliding slickly into Shawn's body, setting him on fire. He knew it wouldn't be a long fuck; he was way too close.

Dave evidently felt the same, suddenly punching his dick harder into Shawn, who put his arms around Dave and tugged him closer, kissing his forehead.

With a growl Dave pushed Shawn onto his back, slipping free of his body briefly, before grabbing hold of Shawn's legs and hooking his arms under the knees. He aimed for Shawn's hole and thrust deep inside him, filling him like he fucking *belonged* there. When Dave began to piston into him, hips slamming into Shawn's arse, Shawn knew they were both about to come.

Dave locked his arms around Shawn's neck and fucked him harder, his cock sliding faster. "Oh, fuck, yeah," he groaned. Shawn reached for his own dick, still free of the panties, and tugged it, working toward his own climax. Above him Dave moved with breathless urgency, so fucking beautiful, his skin gleaming with sweat, mouth wide open, and his eyes focused intently on Shawn's.

And then Shawn was there, coming, shooting his load between them, marking both of them with his spunk.

Dave stilled inside him, bent over, and kissed him with an urgency that stole Shawn's breath. When he broke the kiss, he dragged a finger across Shawn's chest, scooping up some of the cum. He brought the finger to his lips and tasted it, still focused on Shawn.

Then he smiled. "My turn." He caressed Shawn through the silken panties, and Shawn couldn't suppress the shiver that ran the length of his body. Dave smiled. "So fucking sexy."

Shawn grabbed hold of Dave's shoulders and held on as Dave began to move again, quickly picking up speed until he was pistoning in and out of Shawn's body once more.

"Look at me," Dave demanded. "I want you looking at me when I come inside you."

Shawn let out a loud groan as Dave's words sent a fresh pulse of heat flooding through him. Dave thrust once, twice, and then froze above him, his body quivering. Shawn felt the slow throbbing inside him, and *fuck*, that was hot, knowing there were no barriers between them, just skin on skin, Dave's load filling him. Dave sank down on top of him and kissed him, Shawn bringing up his silk-encased legs to wrap them around Dave's waist, crossing them at the ankle.

They lay like that for what seemed ages, Shawn luxuriating in the afterglow of a magnificent fuck. And when Dave finally eased his spent dick from Shawn's body, and asked if he could stay the night, Shawn didn't hesitate.

A night sleeping with Dave, their bodies entwined?

Sounds like heaven.

~ 6 ~

Shawn slipped carefully out of the bed and grabbed his robe from its hook on the back of the bedroom door. He peeked at Dave, but there was no sign of movement from beneath the covers. Shawn glanced at the clock beside his bed, and saw with a shock that it was only six-thirty.

Since when do I wake up this early on a Sunday?

That might have had something to do with the gorgeous man who'd spent the night in his bed. Another glance took in the puddle of silk on the carpet that was the lingerie he'd removed before climbing beneath the sheets.

Yeah. Shawn's stomach tightened, and he hastened from the room, opening and closing the door as quietly as he could.

In the kitchen, he filled the kettle to make coffee, and gazed at the beautiful summer's morning outside his window. It had all the hallmarks of being a lovely day; the sun was already rising in a cloudless sky, and the birds were singing.

Why isn't my heart singing along with them? Because, all things considered, it damn well ought to be.

He'd had sex with Dave. *Dave.* And *God*, such amazing sex too. Dave had turned out to be as considerate in bed as Shawn had imagined, and the way they'd fitted… Perfect.

So what's wrong?

And just like that, Shawn was back to that puddle of silk.

He'd loved every minute of the previous night. He'd never had a partner like Dave, and quite frankly, now that he'd sampled what Dave was capable of, Shawn wanted more. Their sexual chemistry, on top of their friendship, was more than he could ever have hoped for, and Shawn found himself hoping that this could be the start of something. *The start of us.*

Only one thing kept him from doing a happy dance.

He was unsure of Dave's motives. He knew it sounded stupid. He knew he should just be happy that they'd finally ended up fucking. It was just….

Some tiny part of him was concerned that the reason they'd ended up in bed was not so much Dave wanting to fuck *him*, but more a case of Dave being all about the kink. And if that were true, where did that leave Shawn?

Would I be happy to go along with it, if that was the only reason Dave wanted to be with me?

Right then, Shawn didn't know the answer to that particular question.

"Morning." Dave stood in the doorway to the kitchen, yawning and scratching his balls through his T-shirt that just about covered them.

Shawn had to smile and his gaze flickered down to Dave's crotch, before looking him in the eye. "So, this is it then? One night together, and we've already bypassed the social niceties to arrive at the 'scratching my bollocks in front of my partner' stage?" He rolled his eyes. "And to think they said Romance was dead."

Dave snorted, but then he grew still. "Partner?"

Shawn's pulse quickened. "Well, yeah." Inside he wanted to curl up into a tiny ball. *What the hell got into me?* He *never* fucked on a first date. He never just *assumed* that his feelings would be reciprocated. So what made Dave different? What was it about Dave that made Shawn abandon his good sense?

And there was his answer.

It was Dave, pure and simple. The man to whom Shawn had lost his heart so many years ago.

Shawn inhaled deeply and prepared to step off the precipice. "I don't know about you, but I don't let someone in my bed unless I'm... serious about them." He swallowed and hoped to God Dave wasn't about to break his heart less than twelve hours after Shawn had given it to him. Because even if it was Shawn's little kink that drew Dave's interest, Shawn would take it, if it meant he got Dave in his life.

Dave's eyes widened. "Fuck. You think I'd... Fuck, no. I don't just dive into bed with *anyone*, mate." He crossed the kitchen floor in three long strides and took Shawn in his arms. Dave smiled. "I kinda assumed that yeah, we were an item now."

Shawn was glad of Dave's strong arms about him, because right then his legs were shaking. *Thank you, God.* Shawn leaned in and kissed him on the cheek.

Dave frowned. "That's all I get?"

Shawn laughed. "When I've brushed my teeth, there might be more where that came from."

Dave's stomach chose that moment to give a bloody loud rumble, and Dave gave him a sheepish grin. "Maybe after breakfast?"

Shawn could wait that long.

* * * * * *

"So what now?"

Dave cocked his head to one side. "Do you mean once I've finished my coffee? Or are we talking more metaphorically?" His head was full of an idea he'd had when he'd sat up in bed that morning, and glimpsed a pile of black prettiness on the floor. He'd snuck a look at his phone while Shawn was in the bathroom, and all Dave wanted was to get out of there and do some checking out.

Except that leaving had now taken on a new meaning.

Now he would be leaving his… boyfriend.
Fuck. I have a boyfriend.

Shawn chuckled. "I meant, what are you doing with the rest of your Sunday? Did you have any plans before they all got changed because you slept here last night?"

Ahh. Dave seized the opportunity Shawn had just handed him. "Well, now that you mention it, I had a list of things to do today. Much as I've loved spending time with you, I've only really got this afternoon to get shit done."

He hated the way Shawn's expression clicked into neutral, as though he was masking his emotions. *Maybe he is. Maybe he's disappointed. After all, he's just gained a boyfriend too.*

"But," Dave continued quickly, "there's something I'd like us to do next Saturday. It does require some research on my part, however."

"Research?" Shawn's eyes gleamed. "What are you up to?"

Dave grinned. "All shall be revealed." If this fell through, he'd come up with another way to treat Shawn. Except he was *really* hoping it wouldn't. "Unfortunately that means I need to go."

Shawn nodded, only now a hint of sadness had crept into those gorgeous eyes. "I figured. As long as I get to see you next weekend."

Dave knew how to put a smile on his new boyfriend's face. "How about we spend all next weekend together? If we decide to do that, and try to get our usual stuff done during the week…."

It was Shawn's turn to grin. "I like that. And it

will be something to look forward to after a week of slaving over a hot calculator." He winked. "Accountancy humour."

Dave clutched his chest. "Accountants have a sense of humour?"

Shawn narrowed his gaze. "Do you like your balls where they are?" Then he folded his arms across his chest. "And to prove my point.... "

Dave groaned. "No. Please, God, no. Tell me you're not about to bring out a deluge of accountant jokes." His heart soared to see Shawn so relaxed and at ease. *Like we were always meant to be together.* Now that was a sobering thought. *I owe my present happiness to the fact that I flirted with a guy at the gym.*

"All right, you asked for it." Shawn began to walk toward him, eyes locked on Dave. "An accountant is someone who solves a problem you didn't know you had in a way you don't understand."

Dave kept his expression straight. "Please, let me know when you say something funny. I'll tell my face."

Shawn took another step, only now Dave started to back away from him, until the couch hit him in the back of his legs. "Where do homeless accountants live? In a tax shelter."

Dave grimaced. "Ooh. I might have felt a little something then, but.... No."

Shawn arched his eyebrows. "I see." He

pushed Dave down onto the couch, Dave half falling onto it. "Why do economists exist? So that accountants have someone to laugh at."

Dave snorted. "God, you're really bad at this, aren't you?"

At which point Shawn dove on top of him and began tickling him mercilessly. "I'm not admitting defeat yet. I *will* make you laugh, you sod."

"But doing it by tickling… is cheating," Dave gasped out as Shawn's fingers found his ribs. "No! Not there!"

Shawn straddled his waist and reached under his T-shirt to attack Dave's vulnerable spots. "Did you know… a fine is a tax for doing wrong, whereas a tax is a fine for doing well."

"Ooh, ooh, close! I almost smiled." Dave hadn't had this much fun in ages, and the fact that it was with Shawn just made it all the better. "Go on, one more try."

Shawn stilled his fingers and leaned over Dave, who by now was lying stretched out beneath him. "What's the difference between an accountant and a lawyer?" His voice had softened.

Dave pretended to think for a moment. "Okay, I give up."

Shawn smiled. "The accountant *knows* he's boring."

Dave grinned. "Okay, now *that* was funny." Whatever else he'd intended to say was lost when Shawn's mouth met his in a languid kiss that made

Dave warm inside.

Okay, so he didn't have to go *just* yet.

* * * * * *

The glow of the previous weekend had lingered for a couple of days. But then Shawn's initial doubts began to creep back into his mind, even though he'd done his best to ignore them. Not that there hadn't been tiny changes. For one thing, he and Dave had exchanged more texts and messages in one week, than in the previous six months put together. Jokes. Memes. Ideas for future dates. Shawn looked forward to hearing his phone announce each new arrival, and Dave's messages left him in a very good mood.

But as the week wore on, his initial fears had returned, even though there'd been no mention of lingerie in a single message, text or email. Shawn strove to push his panic away, and instead looked forward to discovering Dave's plans for their Saturday.

Whatever he had in mind, Dave was definitely not sharing it. On Saturday morning, when he'd taken Shawn to the city's art gallery, Shawn had been pleasantly surprised—and touched—to find out they were going to look at an exhibition of Pre-Raphaelite paintings. He hadn't even realized Dave knew of Shawn's interest in them, and they spent a couple of hours slowly moving from room to room, while Shawn shared what he knew about his favourite artists.

As they emerged from the gallery, Shawn let out a contented sigh. "That was a lovely surprise. I'd intended going to the exhibition when I first saw it advertised, but you know how things get."

Dave nodded. "Life gets in the way, right?"

"Exactly."

Dave shrugged. "I've seen the books at your place. Plus you have a couple of prints, don't you? So I figured I was on safe ground."

Shawn impulsively leaned across and kissed Dave's cheek, loving the way he flushed and smiled. "Thank you."

Dave grinned, and his mischievous expression set off alarm bells in Shawn's mind. "Glad you liked it. But… that wasn't my surprise."

He stared. "Really?"

"Now we're going to have lunch in a nice little pub in the square, outside where we can people watch and enjoy a beer—or a glass of wine, in your case. And before you ask, that isn't your surprise either. That comes later."

Shawn didn't know what to think. Their first outing together as a couple was exceeding all his expectations, and he was delighted. Even more so when Dave held out his hand. Shawn's heart did a little summersault as he took it, and the pair of them strolled toward the square, hand in hand.

What on earth was I worried about? This was

bliss.

* * * * * *

"Where are you taking me?" Shawn gave his surroundings a doubtful glance. The narrow lanes in the old part of town, with their quaint but expensive designer shops and boutiques, were not his usual shopping ground. They were pretty to look at, all of them set in old buildings that had been lovingly preserved, but as for shopping here? And wherever Dave was taking him had to be near closing, surely; it was already approaching five o'clock. "Are you sure you know where you going?"

Dave chuckled. "When you've quite finished with the twenty questions, we're here." They rounded a corner and—

Shawn gaped. "How did you know about Rosenthals?"

In front of them was a beautiful shop, with large bow windows on either side of an ornate main door. In the window were tasteful displays of lingerie, set on stands or half mannequins, amid a draping of pale lilac satin. Shawn knew the name, of course—he'd seen the shop's website—but it wasn't a place he'd ever visited. Buying online was a lot less problematic. Okay, so he only got to try on the lingerie when it arrived in packages, and that meant the added hassle of returning stuff if it didn't quite fit, but it was preferable to getting weird looks from shop assistants, wondering why this man wanted to take women's lingerie into a fitting room.

Dave led him up to the window and gazed at the pretty displays. "I found this place online. I came here last Sunday after I left your place."

"This... was your research?"

Dave nodded and pointed to the sign in the corner of the window. "What does that say?"

Shawn leaned in to read it. "Open every day, 10.00 - 4.00 or by appointment." He frowned. "By appointment?" Before he could ask anything else, Dave pushed open the door and gestured for him to enter.

They're open? But the sign on the door says Closed. What the hell?

Shawn stepped into the boutique with its heavily varnished wooden floor that spoke of age, its old fashioned wooden display cabinets that somehow seemed perfectly in keeping with the shop, and its several mannequins, draped in various displays of lingerie or nightwear.

A young woman stood behind the glass counter. "Hello, I'm Naomi Rosenthal. You must be Shawn," she said with a smile. She stepped out from behind the counter and walked over to them, her hand extended. They shook hands and she nodded to Dave. "Everything's ready for you." She gave Shawn a quick look up and down. "Yes, you were pretty accurate with the size estimates. If you'll both come this way?"

Shawn gaped. *Size estimates?* This was shaping up to be a day full of surprises, but he couldn't ignore the knot of tension in his belly. *Lingerie*. Just when he'd thought he'd got it all wrong…

"Shawn?"

Shawn surfaced from his uneasy thoughts and blinked.

Dave chuckled. "I know you feel like a kid in a sweet shop right now, but you have a job to do. For one thing, follow the nice lady."

His stomach clenching, Shawn followed Naomi and Dave toward the rear of the shop, where there were two fittings areas, cordoned off with floor length red velvet curtains. She ignored them and instead opened the wooden door to the left of them.

"I've selected five or six items, as we discussed," she said, addressing Dave. "I'll be out here if you need anything else." She gestured for them to step into the room and then closed the door behind them.

Shawn stared at the small, cream-coloured room. To one side was a low, beige leather couch, and to the other, a table and chair. On the wall was a full length mirror, and blinds covered the window. Then his attention went back to the table, where several items lay on top of the crisp white tablecloth.

Time for answers.

He turned to Dave who had already sat on the couch and was leaning back, grinning. "Well? Nice surprise?"

Shawn folded his arms. "What the heck is going on?"

Dave became very still. "I'd have thought that was obvious. When I spoke with Naomi last weekend, she said it was possible to arrange an appointment outside of usual opening hours. She also said she does this a lot for her male customers who come to try on lingerie." When Shawn gaped, he nodded. "Apparently she has quite a few of them. Some come alone, others with their wives or girlfriends. She chooses a selection of lingerie and the customers have time to try them on without feeling embarrassed or nervous." He tilted his head to one side. "So… nice surprise?" His smile had faded, to be replaced by a more careful expression.

Shawn felt like a complete arsehole.

He walked over to where Dave sat and bent down to kiss him. "It's a lovely surprise. Thank you." He ignored the small voice inside his head. *Why did it have to be lingerie though?*

"Why don't you take a look at what she's selected?" Dave suggested.

Shawn went over to the table and peered at the items. He caught his breath at the sight of a teddy, with side panels in a rich deep pink satin, and a central panel in sheer black mesh. Black lace covered the chest area, and when he lifted the padded satin hanger to turn it around, he sighed with pleasure. The back was designed to be worn high, a sheer panel of black mesh, ending in a lace thong.

"This is beautiful."

Dave got up from the couch, walked over to him, and proceeded to help Shawn out of his jacket. "Then try it on." His eyes sparkled. "I'll help."

Shawn wasn't surprised by that last comment. Not one bit. "And you don't think Naomi knows what's going on in here?"

Dave winked. "From the sound of it, this isn't an uncommon occurrence." He leaned in and kissed Shawn on the mouth, then stepped back. "Clothes. Off."

He kicked off his shoes, and Dave undressed him, carefully placing his clothing on the chair. When Shawn was nude, his dick already filling, Dave smiled. "Now. Let's see what you look like." He slipped the beautiful teddy off its hanger and held it out for Shawn to step into it. Dave slowly eased the satiny lingerie up Shawn's body, pausing when he reached his cock. Dave glanced up at Shawn, that mischievous expression back.

Shawn glared. "Don't even think about it," he whispered. "You are *not* giving me a blow job in the middle of a changing room, especially when Naomi is right through that door. And before you even suggest it, no, I don't give a damn how discreet this place is. Got it?"

Dave pouted, and the sight of that full lower lip did not help one little bit. Especially when Shawn could recall vividly how those lips had looked while they were around his—

Stop that. Right now.

Shawn took a deep breath. "Okay. Let's carry on."

Dave nodded and held the straps open so Shawn could slip his arms through them. He adjusted the teddy, making sure it fitted in all the right places, and then looked in the mirror.

"How does it feel?"

Shawn regarded his reflection. It was a good fit, comfortable and not in the least bit tight. The stretchy fabric hugged the contours of his body, and was probably discreet enough to wear beneath his clothes. "It feels great. I feel covered, but then these rear and front panels are see through." He reached behind to where the lace edge went from high on his hip to a thin string between his cheeks. "Love the thong back."

"Yeah, I kinda liked that myself." Dave's hand was suddenly on his arse, stroking the bare flesh. "I see you in this, and all I want to do is spank you in it."

Shawn lifted his eyebrows. "Oh? And how long have you harboured ideas about spanking my arse?"

Dave grinned. "Ever since I saw you in the shower at the gym one time. I thought to myself, 'now there's an arse crying out to be slapped.'" He shifted closer. "Licked." Shawn shivered when Dave's lips brushed his ear. "Bitten."

Holy fuck. Shawn's dick strained against the satin.

Dave stepped back and looked him up and down. "Oh yeah, we're taking this one." He smiled. "How about you try on something else, and then I take you home?"

Another shudder ran through him. "Sure."

Shawn was under no illusions as to what was going to happen once they got there.

~ 7 ~

No sooner were they through Shawn's front door than Dave was propelling him toward the bedroom, jackets already being discarded on the floor. By the time they'd left Rosenthals, Dave's gifts safely stowed under tissue and tape in shiny black bags, Shawn's need had reached burning point. When Dave had suggested taking a taxi home, Shawn knew exactly what had prompted the idea.

It was the fastest means of getting there.

He closed the bedroom door behind them, and seconds later Dave's mouth was on his neck, kissing and licking him there, making him so fucking hard a cat could have used his dick as a scratching post. Fingers fumbled with buttons, hands tugged and pulled, and finally they were both naked, Dave's cock jutting out from his body, thick and pointing toward his navel. Shawn licked his lips, about to sink to his knees and worship it, but Dave stopped him.

"Put it on for me," Dave urged, pointing to the shiny bag on the bed, and Shawn didn't need to ask what he meant. It was on the tip of his tongue to ask if they could just fuck each other's brains out, but part of him was scared that he wouldn't like the answer.

Don't rock the boat. He's here, isn't he? He wants you, doesn't he? So what if he only wants you when you're wearing sexy lingerie? If that's the way things have to be, then put up and shut up.

Shawn was only human after all. He could compromise if that was what it took to keep Dave in his life.

He reached into the bag and removed the tissue-wrapped teddy. His hands shaking, Shawn put it on, aware of Dave's eyes on him the whole time. When he straightened and faced him, his heart pounding, Dave gave a slow nod. "Fucking sexy man. Get on the bed, on all fours. Face the headboard."

Trembling, Shawn obeyed, his breathing rapid, his pulse racing. It was what he'd always wanted, Dave taking charge, being demanding. He hadn't envisaged himself wearing lingerie every time they had sex, however. He got into position and closed his eyes. *Is this how it's always going to be?* And if so, how long would he be prepared to put up with it before he had to say something?

When Dave's cool fingers caressed his arse, Shawn shivered, pushing back into the touch. Warm lips pressed against his skin, gentle kisses that morphed into gentle bites, sending tingles shooting up his spine. And when Dave pulled aside the thong and Shawn felt that first tentative touch of Dave's tongue to his hole, he dropped his head to the bed and moaned.

Dave's breath was warm, but the sudden push of air against the puckered skin was cool. Shawn reached back and spread his cheeks, wanting more. He was rewarded by a hot tongue circling his hole, and when Dave finally pushed the tip inside him, Shawn groaned as a wave of intense pleasure rippled up the length of his body.

"Can't wait. Have to be inside you." Dave was hoarse with desire.

Shawn raised his head and inclined it toward the bedside table. "You know where the lube is." His own voice cracked. He knelt up and pulled apart the velcro fastening to open the teddy, then sank back into position, legs spread wide, waiting.

Dave didn't hang around. Shawn cried out when two slick fingers entered him, pushing back, heedless of the burn. He *needed*, for God's sake. And when the mattress dipped, and a hot, hard, bare cock slowly penetrated him, Shawn forgot his fears, forgot about everything except the man who was making love to him, his hands on Shawn's hips, pulling him back onto Dave's thick shaft.

"Fuck, yeah, that's it. Fuck yourself on my dick." Dave stilled and let Shawn do the work, shoving back, rolling his hips as he impaled himself again and again on that rigid length. Soon they were both moving, Shawn meeting every thrust of Dave's cock deep inside him, bodies slamming together, the loud slap of flesh against flesh so hot and sexy. Dave reached under him to slip a hand between the satin and his skin, wrapping his fingers around Shawn's dick. "Look at you. Sexy as fuck in satin." He filled

Shawn to the hilt with one hard thrust, making Shawn cry out as Dave nailed his gland. "That's the spot, is it?" He pulled all the way out, only to bury his shaft deep once more.

Between the hand on his cock and the other gripping his shoulder, Shawn was pinned. He pushed back onto Dave's thick cock, only to force his own dick through Dave's fist when he pushed forward.

All too soon he felt the tell-tale throb of Dave inside him, and Dave's slick chest against his back as he covered Shawn, kissing him between the straps of the teddy. Shawn groaned at the sensation, Dave's shaft swelling inside him, and tightened his muscles around it. Dave's harsh moan told him how good it felt.

Dave pulled free of him and flipped Shawn onto his back, pulling aside the satin to reveal Shawn's throbbing cock. He cried out when Dave took him deep, sucking hard, his head bobbing as he brought Shawn to orgasm. Shawn grabbed hold of Dave's head and pumped into that hot mouth, hips rocking as he gave up his load. Dave didn't waver for a second, taking every drop of cum that shot from him. When he was truly spent, Shawn let go and melted into the mattress, while Dave crawled up his body to kiss him, sweet, unhurried kisses that bore no relation to the frenzied kisses when they'd first entered the bedroom.

Dave stared into Shawn's eyes. "You are amazing, do you know that?" He stroked Shawn's chest through the layer of lace. "And this? Fuck, this was a damn good idea."

Shawn's scalp prickled and there was a quiver in his stomach. He took a couple of deep, calming breaths and tried to ignore the ache inside him. "I'll be right back." He shifted from beneath Dave and climbed off the bed, heading for the bathroom. Right then he didn't trust himself to stay in that room. *Not if it means I might say something I'll regret.*

Once inside the bathroom he sat on the toilet and put his head in his hands.

Now what do I do? His own reaction told him a lot.

Shawn was apparently no good at compromises.

"Are you okay in there?" Dave's voice was quiet from outside the bathroom door.

He sighed. "I'm fine." He knew he'd have to say something. The only issue now was when.

He glanced down at his body, still encased in the teddy. Shawn pulled it up and over his head, dropping it to the floor. He stared at it, his chest tight.

Fuck, he was a mess.

* * * * * *

Dave was worried. Despite Shawn's denial that something was wrong, Dave trusted his gut instincts, and something was *most definitely* wrong.

They'd gotten dressed, and Shawn had begun making 'what shall we have for dinner' noises, but Dave wasn't fooled. He hadn't missed the sidelong glances when Shawn thought he wasn't looking, or the way Shawn bit his lip.

How many years have I known him? Enough to recognize the signs that said Shawn was not happy. To Dave's mind, such signs after good sex were *not* a good indicator that all was well. He waited until Shawn was peering into cupboards and scanning the contents of the fridge before speaking his mind.

"So, are you going to tell me what's bothering you?"

Shawn stilled, and that neutral expression was back, the one that made Dave's heart sink. Yeah. Something was up.

"It's nothing." Shawn pulled out a box from the cupboard. "I've got some Mediterranean rice—"

"Never mind the fucking rice." Dave yanked the box from his hands and placed it on the counter top. "*Talk* to me, Shawn. I know you, remember? Well enough to know when you're fucking lying to me." Shawn gave him a stricken look, and Dave's brief flare of frustration ebbed away. "I thought we were a couple. Doesn't that mean we talk to each other, share stuff?"

Shawn's eyes widened slightly. Then he bowed his head. "Are we though?"

Dave frowned. "Are we what?"

"A couple."

The barely audible words sent a pang of fear through Dave. "What do you mean?"

Slowly Shawn raised his head and regarded him. "How many times have we had sex?"

Dave did a swift count. "Three."

Shawn nodded in agreement. "And on each of those three occasions, I was wearing lingerie."

Dave nodded, perplexed. He had no clue where this was going.

"Lingerie that *you* asked me to put on," Shawn said pointedly.

"Yeah? Didn't you want to? Is that it? I thought you liked wearing—"

Shawn held up his hand. "Hang on, let me finish." He drew himself up straight. "Did you think about having sex with me before that first time?"

Dave's head was spinning. "Yeah. I thought about it a lot—about you."

Shawn nodded. "But you did nothing about it—until you found my panties. Until you saw me in them."

Cold spread out from Dave's core. "Where are you going with this?"

Shawn sighed. "I don't think what's happening between us is about you and me. It's all about the kink."

Dave was… dumbfounded. "What?"

Shawn shrugged. "I'm sorry, but I had to say something. Don't get me wrong. If it comes down to a choice between not having you in my life, or having you like this—I dress up in lingerie so you want to fuck me—then fine, I'll take you like this. Right now I'll take what I can get."

What. The. Fuck?

Dave inhaled slowly. "I think I've just been insulted."

"I didn't mean it as an insult."

Dave silenced him with a hand held high. "Let me see if I've got this right. You're saying the only reason I like you, the only reason I'm here, is because of the kink." When Shawn didn't respond, but simply stared at him, his face pale, Dave lost his cool. "Did you ever—even once—stop to think that I might like you for *more* than the fact you like to wear sexy lingerie? How long have we been friends? And yet you think I'm just *using* you?" He felt a wave of nausea roll over him. "Forget dinner." He walked out of the kitchen, searching for his jacket.

"Dave. Please, don't leave." Shawn came after him. "I thought—"

Dave whirled around to stare at him. "That's just it. You *didn't* think. Because if you had, you'd have realized how wrong you were." He headed for the door. "See you when I've calmed down."

He was still shaking when he reached his car. Dave got in and leaned back against the head rest. *What the hell?* He searched his feelings, his stomach in turmoil. *Is he right?* He could see why Shawn might have jumped to that conclusion, but still…

He had to get out of there. Because right then

he couldn't think straight.

And there lay the problem. He *wasn't* straight. He was bi, and in love with his best friend. Who had just succeeded in making him doubt himself.

This whole situation was fucked up.

* * * * * *

Shawn was on his third glass of wine by the time his mother called, but it still wasn't enough to dull the ache. Shit, it hadn't even come close.

"'Lo?"

"Shawn? Are you all right? You don't sound yourself."

"Thass cos I'm not. Myself, I mean."

There was a pause. "Baby, what's wrong?"

For one brief moment he considered lying to her, but then he gave up that idea. "You know I said there was someone I was interested in?"

"Yes."

"Well, I thought it was working out, until I had to go and open my big mouth." There'd been nothing from Dave since he'd walked out. Not a single fucking word.

"Aww, sweetheart, what happened?"

Shawn took another gulp of wine before continuing. "I drove him away is the short answer. Cos I was stupid."

Another pause. "Maybe things aren't as bad as you think. Maybe once he's had time to—"

"An' maybe not. I can't afford to think like that. I do that, an' I'll always be waiting, hoping… Thass no way to live." He had to consider an even worse option; Dave staying out of his life completely.

Shit, I really fucked this up, didn't I?

"Don't give up on him, baby."

Shawn snickered. "God, that sounds even cornier than the first time I heard it, listening to your David Soul albums when I was a kid. Sorry, Mum, but I really don't want to talk about this right now. I'll… I'll call you later in the week, all right?"

"Shawn, you listen to me. If this man is meant to be with you, it'll happen. If not, there'll be someone else. I feel it. And when you've found him, you bring him to meet us, and we'll welcome him with open arms." She paused. "Okay?"

He sighed. "Okay. Say hi to Dad for me." He disconnected the call and placed the phone on the cushion beside him, before closing his eyes. He longed to call Dave, to apologize, but knew it was better to let him cool off. Maybe when he'd done that, he'd see things differently. Right then Shawn needed to eat something and lay off the wine, because getting drunk wasn't going to accomplish anything.

Next time I get the urge to say something, I'll keep my big fat mouth shut.

* * * * * *

Dave strained hard, lifting the barbell up to his chest and holding it there for a second before lowering it to the floor.

"How many reps have you done?" a quiet voice asked him.

Dave glanced across at the speaker and bit back his groan. *Go away, Jake. Not now.* Instead he wiped his hands and forehead with his towel and then gave a shrug. "I stopped counting."

Jake nodded, arms folded across his wide chest. "I figured that might be the case. I've been watching you since you got here. I don't know what's going on, but you are pushing yourself way too hard."

"I know what I'm doing." Dave bent his knees and went to pick up the barbell again, but Jake stepped up to him and put his foot on the bar. Dave glared at him. "Off. Now."

Jake shook his head. "Not until you tell me what's wrong. You're overdoing it, and it's not like you. At this rate you're going to do yourself an injury."

"It's personal. Back off."

Jake still hadn't removed his foot. "Nope. Not until you talk to me."

Dave sighed heavily and straightened. "None. Of. Your. Business." He pulled off his tank top and wiped himself down.

Jake stepped back, studying him closely. "It's

a guy, isn't it?"

Dave blinked. "What?"

Jake smiled, his eyes kind. "I've been there, mate."

"Not your mate."

"Maybe not, but right now you need one, and I don't see anyone else around here offering their ear for you to bend, right? So you'll have to make do with me." Jake inclined his head toward the locker room. "Come on. We can sit and you can tell me what's happened. I swear, just a chat. I think you need to. A problem shared, and all that."

Dave huffed. "Not gonna get rid of you, am I?"

Jake beamed. "*Now* you're getting it." He pointed to the locker room. "Lead the way."

Shaking his head, Dave exited the weights room and headed for the lockers. There was no one around, but the gym had only been open a couple of hours, and Sunday mornings were always quiet.

Can't see me working out on a Sunday morning with Shawn for a while. The thought left him with an ache in his chest.

They sat on the wooden bench, Jake astride it, his hands resting on his chunky thighs. "Okay, spill."

Dave began at the beginning, and finished at the moment where he'd walked out of Shawn's flat. "I thought I was being supportive, you know, showing him that it really didn't bother me if that's what he was into. Turns out he thought he was being used."

Jake pursed his lips. "I can see where Shawn's coming from though."

Dave gaped. "You what?"

Jake shrugged. "Nah, it makes sense. Why wouldn't he think that? The only time you showed an interest in getting intimate was when you had him put on his silky stuff. It adds up." When Dave opened his mouth to retort, Jake held up a finger. "I'm not saying he's right. I'm just saying that when you look at it, that's the assumption *I'd* come to as well. So let me ask you a question. What if Shawn stopped wearing lingerie? For ever? Would that change the way you feel about him?"

Dave didn't hesitate. "Not for a fucking millisecond. I… love him."

Jake gave a slow smile. "Then do something about it. You've told *me* how you feel—but have you told him?" When Dave opened and closed his mouth, Jake shook his head. "Bloody typical. Why is it that as a species, men are crap at communication? We never say what's on our minds, and it leads to all kinds of problems. So do yourself a favour, and go see that mate—that *boyfriend*, I should say—of yours, and sort this out. And the next time I see you, the two of you had better be looking all loved up. I'll be so relieved, I won't even take the piss out of you." He winked. "Maybe." He flicked Dave with his towel. "Get showered, then get your fine arse round to Shawn's." When Dave arched his eyebrows, Jake chuckled. "A man can look, can't he? Now get a bloody move on."

Dave stood and on impulse, held out his hand. "Thanks, Jake."

Jake rose to his feet, ignoring it, and gave Dave a hug. "Think nothing of it. As long as you know you're gonna ache like a bastard later. You really did push too hard. I was worried." As Dave headed to his locker to grab his toiletries, Jake stopped him. "And Dave? You've got me for a friend, all right?" He grinned. "Even if you *do* have questionable taste in men."

Dave stuck two fingers up at him, laughing. "Bastard."

Jake flexed, his muscles rippling. "Hey, this could have been yours, but *noooo*, you want Shawn. Your loss, mate."

Dave shook his head, still chuckling as he entered the showers. "I think I'll live," he called out as he flipped on the jets. He closed his eyes and let the water sluice away his bodily aches.

Then I'll go deal with the one in my heart.

~ 8 ~

Shawn dragged his clothes from the drier and began to fold them automatically, his mind not really on his laundry. After all, that was how this whole mess had started, right? Damn Dave and his wanting to help. If he hadn't looked in that bloody drawer…

Shawn sighed. *If he hadn't looked in that drawer, I wouldn't have experienced the best sex in my life so far, and that wonderful feeling I got when I thought he loved me.* It didn't matter what had happened the previous day. Shawn knew deep down that he loved Dave, and that wasn't about to change. He only hoped that once the waters had settled, he and Dave could still be friends.

That's if I haven't driven him away for good.

The ping of his phone in the living room served as a welcome distraction from such thoughts. Shawn abandoned the riveting task of laundry folding and went to find out who was texting him. When he saw the screen, all the hairs on the back of his neck stood on end.

Can we talk?

On the one hand, he was overjoyed that Dave wanted them on speaking terms, but on the other? Shawn dreaded what he might hear when they were face-to-face. Not enough to put Dave off, though.

Sure. Phone or in person?

A moment later he had his answer. *On my way.*

Shawn glanced at his reflection in the mirror on the wall. He looked okay, if a little tired. Unsurprisingly, sleep had been particularly elusive.

This time it appeared Dave hadn't been waiting just around the corner. A good thirty minutes had elapsed before Shawn caught the familiar noise of Dave's car pulling up in the street below. Shawn had boiled the kettle ready for coffee, and a plate of chocolate biscuits sat on the coffee table. *Talk about déjà vu.*

Shawn opened the door and left it on the latch, before nipping into the kitchen to make the coffee.

"Hi, it's only a burglar," Dave called out.

Shawn had to smile. *He really does know me.* "In the kitchen." His heart pounded, and he did his damnedest to breathe evenly, but *fuck*, he was nervous. He didn't turn around as Dave entered the room. "Just making coffee. And there are biscuits on the table."

"Shawn?"

He took one more hopefully calming breath and turned to face Dave, who stood in the doorway, a flat white box in his hand. Shawn's heart plummeted at the sight of it. *No change there then.*

"Hey there." Shawn forced a smile. "Let me take your jacket. Unless you're not stopping?"

"That sort of depends on you." Dave scraped a hand through his curly hair. "I've been thinking about what you said yesterday."

Shawn went back to making the coffee. "Oh?" His heart was still hammering.

"I wanted to bring you a gift, and I really struggled to come up with the right thing for you. But in the end, I think I nailed it."

Shawn turned around to find Dave holding out the white box. He took it, his hands trembling.

"I think this is perfect for you." Dave gave a shaky smile. "I'm hoping you feel the same way."

Shawn was almost too afraid to look.

Almost.

He lifted the lid, and something deep in his belly rolled over at the sight of layers of tissue. Still, he peeked under them and found—

What the fuck?

The only item in the box was a photo. Shawn grabbed hold of it and placed the box on the counter top. It was of him and Dave, in their final year in high school, taken the night of the school prom. Both of them had hired tuxedos for the night. It was an event Shawn would never forget. The sight of Dave, resplendent in his smart attire, had made him acutely aware of his feelings for him.

Feelings that hadn't changed one iota.

There had been casual boyfriends, but nothing that had lasted beyond a month. Shawn had always known he could never have the one person he truly loved, and had made a real effort to find someone, but somehow it had never happened for him.

He raised his chin and stared at Dave. "I don't

understand."

Dave smiled. "I said I'd found something that was perfect for you, right? Well, here it is. Me. *I'm* perfect for you, Shawn, because... I love you." He gestured toward the empty box. "There's no pretty lingerie in there, and there never has to be. If you told me you were never going to wear it again, I wouldn't bat an eyelid. But if you told me you were never going to see me again? That I *couldn't* live with." He took a step closer. "So let me say it again. I love you. I don't want to lose you. And I need to know if you love me too."

Shawn's throat tightened. He gazed at the photo in his hand and smiled. Finally the words came.

"You see the goofy look on my face here? Do you know *why* I looked like that? Because I was looking at the boy who'd stolen my heart. A boy who could never love me back the way I wanted him to, because he wasn't gay." Shawn smiled. "So you can imagine how I felt when you suddenly announced that you're bi-sexual."

Dave grinned. "You thought Christmas had come early?"

Shawn laughed and launched himself across the room and into Dave's waiting arms. "All my Christmases yet to come," he whispered. He looked Dave in the eye and smiled. "I love you too."

Dave shuddered out a long breath, and then his lips were on Shawn's, his hands caressing his back, his shoulders, everywhere. They kissed until Shawn couldn't take it anymore.

"Can we continue this conversation somewhere else?"

Dave curved a hand around Shawn's cheek. "How about in bed?" he said softly.

Shawn let out a supremely contented sigh. "Perfect." He placed the photo on top of the box and led Dave out of the kitchen and toward his bedroom.

"By the way," Dave said as Shawn closed the door behind them. "Do you know what I'd like to see you in?" When Shawn gave him an inquiring glance, he grinned. "Absolutely nothing."

Shawn thought that sounded like a wonderful idea.

* * * * * *

"Are you sure this is a good idea, turning up out of the blue?"

Shawn chuckled. "Trust me. Mum will be delighted to see me. And as for me bringing you? Wait and see." He came to a halt at the front door.

Dave bit his lip. "Don't get me wrong. I love your mum like she was my own, always have done, but she never struck me as the sort of person who took well to having surprise guests sprung on her."

Shawn leaned over and kissed him on the lips. "We'll see." He slipped his key into the lock and let them into the house. "Only us burglars!"

"Shawn? Why didn't you tell me you were—" Mum flung open the kitchen door and stopped dead. "Dave! Oh, how nice. We haven't seen you for ages." She glared at Shawn. "I *do* have a phone, you know. You might have given me some notice."

"See?" Dave murmured beside him.

Shawn ignored him and reached for his hand, lacing their fingers together. "Mum? We have something to tell you."

Mum's gaze dropped instantly to their joined hands, and to his surprise, her eyes grew sparkly. She wiped them quickly with the tea towel she was holding, and then beamed at them.

"Well, it's about bloody time!"

Shawn blinked. Blinked again. Beside him, Dave burst out laughing.

"And now that you've both finally got your heads out of the sand and come to your senses," Mum said, recovering swiftly, "you can march into my kitchen and help me with the dinner. *After* you've made me a cocktail." She grinned and promptly disappeared back into the kitchen. "And go find your dad. He's in the back garden," she called out.

Shawn leaned into Dave and whispered. "This could turn out to be a long night."

Dave surprised the hell out of him by kissing him on the lips. "It's okay. I'll be right here beside you."

Shawn couldn't resist. "I did plan a surprise

for when we got back to my place, to say thank you for agreeing to this."

"Oh?" Dave's eyes gleamed.

Shawn tugged at his jeans, pulling the waistband a little lower.

Dave grinned. "Aw, the polka dot ones. My favourite."

Shawn had a feeling his prediction for a long night ahead was going to come true.

The End

Coming Soon…
Before You Break (With Parker Williams, Secrets #1) from Dreamspinner Press. Coming May 26, 2017

Six years ago Ellis walked into his first briefing as the newest member of London's Specialist Firearms unit. He was partnered with Wayne and they became fast friends. When Wayne begins to notice changes—Ellis's erratic temper, the effects of sleep deprivation—he knows he has to act before Ellis reaches breaking point. He invites Ellis to the opening of the new BDSM club, Secrets, where Wayne has a membership. His purpose? He wants Ellis to glimpse the lifestyle before Wayne approaches him with a proposition. He wants to take Ellis in hand, to control his life because he wants his friend back, and he figures this is the only way to do it.

There are a few issues, however. Ellis is straight. Stubborn. And sexy. Wayne knows he has to put his own feelings aside to be what Ellis needs. What surprises the hell out of him is finding out what Ellis actually requires.

Out of The Shadows (A Dreamspun Desires novel)

Can he step out of the shadows and into love's light?

Eight years ago, Christian Hernandez moved to Jamaica Plain in southern Boston, took refuge in his apartment, and cut himself off from the outside world. And that's how he'd like it to stay.

Josh Wendell has heard his coworkers gossip about the occupant of apartment #1. No one sees the mystery man, and Josh loves a mystery. So when he is hired to refurbish the apartment's kitchen and bathrooms, Josh is eager to discover the truth behind the rumors.

When he comes face-to-face with Christian, Josh understands why Christian hides from prying eyes. As the two men bond, Josh sees past his exterior to the man within, and he likes what he sees. But can Christian find the courage to emerge from the darkness of his lonely existence for the man who has claimed his heart?

When Christian appeared in the doorway, dressed in faded jeans and a long-sleeved shirt, Josh blinked. "Isn't it a little warm for long sleeves?" He already had an inkling why Christian had chosen to wear it, but he was determined to show him he had nothing to fear.

Christian seemed to consider his words. After a moment, he nodded. "Maybe you're right." He disappeared again, and Josh got on with making the coffee. When Christian reappeared, this time wearing a dark green T-shirt that hugged his contours, Josh wanted to stare for a whole new set of reasons. Christian's toned arms. Christian's *abs*.

Think he'd notice if I started drooling? He gave an internal grin. *I could always blame it on the croissants.*

Christian walked over to where he stood, not meeting Josh's gaze. Whatever small measure of triumph Josh had experienced at having Christian join him evaporated.

We've clearly got a long way to go until he feels comfortable around me. Not that they had time to do that. It wouldn't be long before Josh was finished, and then he'd be out of there.

Then I'll have to work fast, won't I?

Josh loved a challenge. And he wasn't thinking about the kitchen.

Available August 2017

By K.C. Wells

<u>Learning to Love</u>
Michael & Sean
Evan & Daniel
Josh & Chris
Final Exam

Love lessons Learned
A Bond of Three
Le lien des Trois
A Bond of Truth
First
Debt
Dette
Il Debito
Waiting for You
The Senator's Secret
Step by Step

<u>Collars & Cuffs</u>
An Unlocked Heart
Trusting Thomas
Someone to Keep Me
(K.C. Wells & Parker Williams)
A Dance with Domination
Damian's Discipline
(K.C. Wells & Parker Williams)
Make Me Soar
Dom of Ages

(K.C. Wells & Parker Williams)
Endings and Beginnings
(K.C. Wells & Parker Williams)

Un Coeur Déverrouillé

<u>Personal</u>
Making it Personal
Personal Changes
More than Personal
Personal Secrets
Strictly Personal
Personal Challenges

Une Affaire Personnelle
Changements Personnels
Plus Personnel
Secrets Personnels
Strictement Personnel

Una Questione Personale
Cambiamenti Personali
Piú che personale
Segreti Personali
Strettamente personale

Es wird persönlich
Persönliche Veränderungen
Mehr als Persönliche
Persönliche Geheimnisse

LACE

Streng Persönlich

Confetti, Cake & Confessions
Confetti. Coriandoli e Confessioni

Connections
Connexion

Saving Jason

Island Tales

Waiting for a Prince
September's Tide
Submitting to the Darkness

Le Maree di Settembre
In Attesa di un Principe

Lightning Tales
Teach Me
Trust Me
See me
Love Me

Lehre Mich
Vertau Mir

Double or Nothing

K.C. Wells

Back from the Edge
Switching it up

<u>Anthologies</u>

<u>Fifty Gays of Shade</u>
Winning Will's Heart

Who is Tantalus?

For those who like their stories intensely erotic, featuring hot men and even hotter sex….

Who don't mind breaking the odd taboo now and again….

Who want to read something that adds a little heat to their fantasies….

…there's Tantalus.

Because we all need a little tantalizing.

Tantalus is the hotter, more risqué alter ego of K.C. Wells

<u>Playing with Fire (Damon & Pete)</u>

A series of (so far) four short gay erotic stories:

- Summer Heat
- After
- Consequences
- Limits

About the Author

K.C. Wells started writing in 2012, although the idea of writing a novel had been in her head since she was a child. But after reading that first gay romance in 2009, she was hooked.

She now writes full time, and the line of men in her head, clamouring to tell their story, is getting longer and longer. If the frequent visits by plot bunnies are anything to go by, that's not about to change anytime soon.

E-mail: **k.c.wells@btinternet.com**

Facebook: **https://www.facebook.com/KCWellsWorld**

Twitter: @K_C_Wells

Website: **http://www.kcwellsworld.com**

Instagram: https://www.instagram.com/k.c.wells/

Printed in Great Britain
by Amazon